A SOJOURN AMONG THE AVATARS OF WISDOM

A Novella

DUDLEY MECUM

A SOJOURN AMONG THE AVATARS OF WISDOM

iUniverse books may be ordered through booksellers or by contacting:

iUniverse LLC
1663 Liberty Drive
Bloomington, IN 47403
www.iuniverse.com
1-800-Authors (1-800-288-4677)

ISBN: 978-1-4620-2524-4 (sc)
ISBN: 978-1-4620-2525-1 (e)

Printed in the United States of America.

iUniverse rev. date: 11/02/2015

COVER CREDITS:
Front cover artwork created by artist Dennis Soultaire, Fort Worth, Texas
"Great Sword of War" designed by Michael "Tinker" Pierce
Cover photo provided by CAS Iberia

CONTENTS

CHAPTER 1

A CELESTIAL RIOT

Amid the great expanse of the star-filled sky, light from the crescent moon reflects off the warm, undulating surf. A humid, early September breeze sweeps on shore past a beach strewn with scattered seashells, pebbles, and an occasional stranded jellyfish. Beyond the hardwood hammock-filled spit of land lie partially submerged alligators in a lagoon, waiting for their next meal. A symphony of frogs and crickets fills the early evening air. Centered in a vast circular clearing a half mile inland, a spotlight-illuminated launch complex erupts with an ominous rumbling.

Abruptly shockwaves ripple outward as ephemeral walls of condensation travel at the speed of sound, heralding a blinding burst of light and a volcanic roar. Two immense jets of flame scorch the earth in opposite directions and then quickly recede, growing into twin pillars of fire. Night turns to day briefly as the earth shudders like an earthquake. Vaulting above the banks of billowing exhaust clouds, that celestial dart known as the space shuttle, centered on an orange external fuel tank and flanked by two white solid rocket boosters, thunders heavenward.

Like a giant yellow flare piercing the night sky, the orbiter's burning exhaust traces a gentle arc over the Atlantic Ocean. Inside

1

the spacecraft six crew members are all wearing pumpkin-colored pressure suits, their dark visors on their white helmets locked in the down position. Not only do the astronauts feel seismic vibrations coursing through the shuttle but also a heaviness against their chests from being hurled at up to three times the force of gravity, which their G suits counteract to a limited degree.

The orbiter's cockpit-like flight deck, covered in a sea of buttons, knobs, and switches, would intimidate any 747 captain. Unlike a conventional airplane, the spacecraft has over two thousand controls and displays for space, conventional atmospheric, and payload operations.

Commander Susan Wells and pilot Xavier Howard monitor their ascent as three hundred black boxes connected to five general-purpose computers ensure that the shuttle is on the correct trajectory.

Sitting behind the commander and pilot, Chris Cole, a payload specialist and the final crew member on the flight deck, revels in his first launch. His duties will begin at the midpoint of the mission.

Also onboard are three members of the next expeditionary crew to the International Space Station, who are seated on the middeck, one level below the cockpit.

Just two minutes into its eight-and-a-half-minute climb to orbit, the spacecraft automatically jettisons its twin 150-foot solid rocket boosters, momentarily making the orbiter appear as a rising comet, while inside the flight deck, the astronauts see a blinding flash.

The shuttle's ride instantly becomes smoother as the solid rocket boosters fall away at an altitude of 150,000 feet. The orbiter's progressively horizontal trajectory continues until it is nearly flat, inverting the spacecraft. Even though the astronauts are seated normally, their heads point toward the sea.

The shuttle, rocketing northeast over the North Atlantic toward dawn over Europe, slices through an ever-thinning atmosphere, which provides less of a medium in which to propagate sound, over the course of the next six and a half minutes. As a result, the roar of the main engines gradually abates.

Near the end of the ascent, the orbiter slowly rolls to a normal heads-up position. Reaching a speed of roughly 17,500 miles per hour in a little more than eight minutes, the spacecraft reaches main engine cutoff, and everyone experiences weightlessness. So fast is the shuttle's speed that it circles the globe once every ninety minutes, reducing day and night to forty-five minutes each.

Earth, looming beyond the cockpit windows, casts a lustrous cerulean hue against the unforgiving black void of space. Adding to the unnaturalness of space flight is traversing entire continents in minutes, unified without national borders.

The welcome quiet, save for the whir of the avionics, is interrupted by a clanging sound of the jettisoned external fuel tank, which will eventually break up as it reenters the atmosphere over the Indian Ocean. Minutes later Susan spots the spent fifteen-story orange external fuel tank, which is blackened on the top third of the structure from explosive jettison charges, floating forlornly in space.

Secured inside and occupying one third of the orbiter's cargo bay is the multipurpose logistics module, a metallic cylindrical container used to transfer supplies and equipment to the International Space Station. Also stowed as cargo is Chris's payload—a pair of soccer ball-sized, tethered, self-propelled satellites that will eventually provide permanent remote video inspection of the same facility, which he will deploy on day two of the mission.

As the spacecraft approaches the terminator line that divides day from night, towering thunderheads brushed with coral tones—their shadows slanting across the sea—swiftly scroll into view. Farther to the east Earth dissolves into darkness. Pulses of light flicker in the distance, which, as the shuttle draws closer, gradually blossom into massive storms with volleys of lightning arcing through a network of clouds.

Soon nature's fireworks disappear from view. And where the clear skies dominate the land, a strange web of lights shines forth, with many bright strands clustered along the coast and pale threads stretched inland. Then a sea of darkness reigns again until a glowing orange crescent forms on the horizon, for the orbiter is nearing the terminator line once more as dawn approaches.

The light of a new day rapidly washes over the spacecraft and veils the heavens. But on the horizon a lone starlike object remains— the crew's new home, the International Space Station (ISS), orbiting 240 miles above Earth.

A model of equanimity with olive eyes and shoulder-length black hair, Susan Wells, forty-seven, is commanding her second mission. One of the few female astronauts to lead a space flight, she attained a bachelor's degree in physics and astronomy from Wellesley College and acquired a master of science in aerospace engineering at the Georgia Institute of Technology.

Xavier Howard, to her right, is an African American of forty-two with a low-cut fade. Climbing NASA's corporate ladder, he obtained a bachelor's degree in aeronautical and astronautical engineering from Purdue University and achieved a master of science in flight structures engineering at Columbia University. The pilot is not only responsible for assisting the commander during the mission but also for making sure that the landing gear is down and locked shortly before landing.

Payload specialist Chris Cole belongs to a designation of noncareer astronauts tasked with the successful deployment of their companies' experiments, which requires one or two missions at most. Upon the completion of their objectives, those professionals return to their old jobs. He trained three months for this mission.

Chris, who is forty-one, has gentle, wavy sandy-brown hair, graying temples, kind brown eyes, and a reassuring voice.

Peering through the left overhead window at the space station, Susan admires the ISS—a pressurized gold-and-silver redoubt whose living space is many times larger than that of the shuttle's. Cast against the bleakness of space, the half-completed space station is an odd-looking home for the astronauts. Except for the solar arrays and the airlock chamber, the structure would fit inside a general outline of a submarine.

After an interminable approach many times longer than that of its ascent, the orbiter finally docks, which goes unnoticed by the passengers on the middeck.

Susan breathes a sigh of relief, as her duty as commander—charged with the success and safety of flying NASA's two-billion dollar spaceship—has been successfully discharged on this leg of the trip but will resume again on the return stage several days hence.

* * *

The crew, having shed their bulky pressure suits and donned their more comfortable sneakers and cotton shirts and shorts, follows Susan through the spacious airlock chamber. She removes and stows the station's inner airlock seal and emerges from a circular hatch at the front of the space station, where she meets the current ISS crew members. In keeping with tradition, one member of the hosting crew rings in each new visitor.

CHAPTER 2

LIFE AMONG SUPERHEROES

Sensory overload greets Chris's eyes as he deposits himself in the space station. Equipment racks, each with their own sets of controls, line not only the walls but also the ceiling and floors. Laptops spring from the walls. Monitors abound above jutting workstations from which writhing cable wires sprout like roots, and the hum of ventilation fans drones in the background.

Brian Thomas, the current ISS commander, whose chiseled face could easily lead one to believe that he was former football player, radiates an abundance of confidence acquired from hundreds of aircraft flights, several prior shuttle missions, a previous Expedition experience as a flight engineer, and years of training, Chris remembers from reading the astronaut's bio. Brian briskly floats toward Susan and gives her a brief hug. "Great to see you!" he says. "Welcome aboard."

"Glad to see you and the rest of your crew," Susan says.

Extending an open palm to his right, Brian says, "As you know, Leslie Kessler and Nikolai Panin are the current flight engineers."

"Nice to meet you," Susan says and shakes their hands. Gesturing to her right, Susan says, "I would like to introduce you to Xavier Howard, our pilot, and Chris Cole, our payload specialist. And the replacement crew, ISS Commander Sergei Antipov and flight engineers Karen Hastings and Gregory Sentilles."

Following the obligatory handshaking, Brian informs Susan, "You launched in a nick of time. A tropical disturbance passed West Palm Beach about seven hours ago and is moving toward Kennedy Space Center. It's almost as if the weather system is riding the Gulf Stream northward along the coast. In fact, the National Hurricane Center is predicting that it will continue on its present course."

"Yes, I was briefed on its location," Susan says. "Fortunately we had clear skies and calm weather, so we were able to launch. But that thunderstorm complex is moving fast."

"At least you don't have to worry about the weather up here," Brian says, arching an eyebrow.

"Yes, that's one less thing to worry about," Susan says with a subtle nod.

"I don't think any of your crew members have seen the place," Brian says. "I'm sure everyone needs some time to unwind. Would you like to stretch your legs now that you're here and take a tour of the facilities, not an underwater mock-up?"

"Sure," Susan says crisply. She turns to the rest of her crew and announces, "Listen up! Brian has volunteered to give us a tour, so please pay attention. Thank you."

With gravity absent, a few of the crew members gather near the ceiling. Some secure themselves to a wall, and the rest cling to the floor. In fact, *up* is a relative term in space. Only the orientation of the equipment along the walls and the placards on the forward and aft bulkheads artificially determines direction.

Hovering in the middle of the module and facing the newcomers, Brian rubs his jaw for several moments and then says, "Welcome aboard. Glad you could make it here. Visitors don't come knocking on our door that often." That elicits a few chuckles. "Although we are far from completing this place, you'll be glad to know that your new home is several times larger than the livable space on the shuttle. In fact, the living pressurized volume here is eighteen hundred square feet, equivalent to a three-bedroom house. Did you know that, Chris?"

"Any vessel that is larger than the orbiter would be a welcome relief," Chris says.

"But if you spent six months up here in space," Brian corrects, "this place would seem quite small! It would have been nice to have all the modules currently assembled. But since the shuttle can only bring up one module at a time, it will take several years to complete the space station, and our mission would have ended long before then."

Pointing to Chris with an open palm, Brian asks, "Would you like to know how your tax dollars are being spent to support NASA's permanent human presence in space?"

"Sure," Chris says.

Midway through Brian's explanation of the various refrigerator-sized equipment racks lining the floor, ceiling, and walls, Chris interrupts. "You've got all this equipment up here that's great for scientists," he says. "But what can the general public look forward to?"

"I see what interests you," Brian says with a slight nod of his head. "We conduct experiments that will improve the treatment of heart disease, cancer, osteoporosis, diabetes, and anemia. On that note, I'll wrap it up by mentioning just two more things that might interest you."

Pointing to the crew's right, Brian says, "Over here is one of a few laptops scattered throughout the modules that displays a diagram of the space station. Through a series of mouse clicks, you can control the electrical flow throughout all the modules. As a result, there are no manual circuit breakers.

"Finally," Brian says, pointing beneath him, "if you peer into the rack-sized gap in the middle of the floor, you'll see a twenty-inch window, the largest one in the space station, from which you can film—either high-quality video or still photography—such spectacles as floods and wildfires, plankton blooms, hurricanes, and coral reefs.

"But it's not all work up here," Brian continues, glancing at his watch. "I had a chance to plot our course before you arrived, and our orbit should take us southeast over the Himalayas. Hopefully the monsoons have ended, and you'll have a good chance to look at the mountain range.

"Chris, since this will be your only visit here, you get the privilege of viewing the region first."

Obliging, Chris floats over to the floor window, gazes through, and only sees a blanket of clouds. His chance to see the "roof of the world" will have to wait for another day, and he sighs.

To allow the others to take their turn to look, Chris returns to his original place.

"Why do you look so sad?" Leslie asks.

"Oh," Chris says, caught off guard. "It's a long story. Some other time."

"All right," she says, shrugging. "If you didn't like what you saw out the window, perhaps you'll like what I've got in store for you next. The equipment rack on the floor near the forward end of the module—the same direction as the docked shuttle—failed this morning, and I'll need to troubleshoot it. Since you are the junior person onboard, you can help Nikolai remove the apparatus from its cradle by grabbing the blue handle near the starboard side of the unit. Then the two of you can pivot the equipment rack upright as if it were hinged on its port side."

"I'll bet the unit is heavy if it's just as big as the others," Chris ventures as he and Nikolai float over to the defective apparatus.

"The two of you will manage," Leslie says, who is a former navy pilot, Chris recollects from reading her biography of the current Expedition crew. Her vermillion hair is held tightly in place by a matching colored hair clip, her skin pale and her eyes resolute— probably gained from landing hundreds of times on a "postage stamp" runway on a rolling carrier deck at sea in occasional difficult conditions in which no alternate landing site exists, Chris imagines.

"How much does this weigh?" Chris asks as a sense of doubt grips him.

"Oh, about 1,200 pounds," Leslie says.

"I hope you're right about my strength," Chris says.

"Don't worry," Leslie says. "I helped install the equipment rack six months ago."

"Really?" Chris says incredulously. "Well, here we go," he says as he and Nikolai strain to lift the refrigerator-sized unit out of its cradle. Slowly the apparatus rises from the floor just as Leslie described.

"Don't move it out too fast," Leslie cautions. "Remember, that piece of equipment will have a lot of momentum." As they hoist the equipment rack's starboard edge to shoulder-level, she says, "That's enough. Nikolai and I will do the rest."

Beaming, Chris releases the unit as Nikolai steadies it. "Wow, I am like Superman up here!" Chris exclaims.

"We're all like Superman in space," Brian says, his expression becoming more serious, "but we grow weaker by the day in weightlessness. In fact, if your mission were to last a year, you wouldn't have the strength to stand up upon your return home because of bone and muscle loss. You'd be the weakest person on Earth! That's why we only stay up here for six months, even with fifty minutes of cardio activity and a half hour of resistance training every day. Who knew that gravity would be so beneficial?"

"Someone should take Chris's picture," Leslie suggests. "It's all downhill from here!"

Immediately, Karen retrieves a small digital camera from the case secured to her belt and snaps a photo of the payload specialist, who strikes his best superhero pose with one hand on his hip and the other shading his eyes, half-expecting to see trouble on the horizon.

Leslie informs Brian, "Nikolai and I will troubleshoot the defective rack's power source now that it's out of its cradle. Give us about fifteen minutes, and then we'll rejoin you."

"All right," Brian says, nodding. Addressing the rest of the crew members, he says, "That completes the explanation of this module. Now if you'll follow me."

Brian leads everyone aft, passing through the hatch opening that leads to the *Unity* node, a six-sided connecting hub to which other modules are attached. Chris enters the *Unity* node last and is impressed with its spaciousness. Behind him is the passageway back to the US laboratory. In front of him is a hatch opening that's centered in the coral-colored bulkhead, leading to the first of two Russian modules, Chris remembers from his training courses. Off to his left is the airlock chamber where astronauts assemble before the compartment is depressurized, allowing them to begin their space walk.

As Brian points out areas of interest to the rest of the crew, Chris looks around the cube-like chamber, whose interior is lined with padded white rectangular storage bags. The module's exterior measures fifteen feet in diameter and eighteen feet in length, he recollects from his astronaut training, and it has the largest vertical and horizontal clearances in the station. Chris surveys the interior for fun possibilities.

Seizing the opportunity, he floats over to Brian and asks, "Since this will be my only time in space, can you let me soar from the floor to the ceiling and back?"

"If you need to work out, there's a resistance exercise device on the ceiling where you can do squats. Or you can run on the treadmill a few modules aft," Brian suggests, motioning to both locations.

"No, my heart is set on this—something that I've wanted to do since I was a kid," Chris admits.

"Sure," Brian says. "Suit yourself." Turning to the other crew members, he announces, "Okay everyone. Let's give Chris some room. Unfortunately he left his cape at home!"

To accommodate the payload specialist, everyone else moves to one side of the *Unity* module. Feeling like a kid again, Chris takes advantage of his newfound playground. It takes the same amount of effort to float five feet or to soar to the ceiling. Only the confines of the station limit his achievements.

Brian asks Leslie, "Doesn't he look taller?"

"Not yet," Leslie says, breaking into a mischievous grin.

"What's this talk about my height?" Chris asks, who glides back to the floor.

"You might have grown an inch or two taller in space," Brian says. "In weightlessness your spine is no longer compressed. But don't worry. You won't become a giant."

"I wouldn't mind being one right now," Chris says. "I could easily defeat all my enemies back on Earth."

"You look tall enough to me," Brian says. "Hopefully your increased height will not prevent you from squeezing through the aft passageway. Are you claustrophobic?"

"Don't worry," Chris assures, waving his hand dismissively.

"Good," Brian says. "Now follow me." In short order, he disappears through the hatch opening, which looks like a giant inverted throat on the far wall. The rest of the crew members follow him one by one, with Chris bringing up the rear.

* * *

Chris squeezes out of the torpedo tube-sized forward hatch opening that's centered midway up the wall where the two modules are joined together. He propels himself along two vertically aligned, inclined handles secured to a rising platform above which the stowed hatch looms—suspended at least a foot beneath the ceiling. Snuggled below the hatch opening, a bank of laptop workstations rises up from the floor.

Like the shape of a giant telescope, the module's interior, split by the floor, expands abruptly midway toward the aft end. Studying the surface immediately below him more closely, Chris recognizes the apparent verdure rust-proofing sealant is a faux reminder of grass underfoot, now hundreds of miles beneath him.

Taken as a whole, a dizzying array of equipment— communications, life support, food service, flight control, and data processing—hugs the walls. One of the laptops in the workstations below him controls electrical power distribution, its display similar to the laptop screen that Brian had pointed out and explained earlier.

Absent are the familiar objects of home—wallpaper, windows along the walls, carpeting, and seating of any kind. Thankfully a smooth ceiling adds some sense of normalcy to the crew's biosphere.

As Chris slowly makes his way aft, Brian motions him to hurry up and adds, "Good. We haven't lost anyone yet.

"Since we are resupplied about once a month, it's more practical to have the food canned or already cooked and then dehydrated and stored in vacuum-sealed containers to be reconstituted and microwaved when needed.

"To prevent bone and muscle loss during our six-month stay, we use a treadmill that's flush with the floor and adjacent to the crew table, centered in the aft part of the module. Naturally anyone using it would have to be held down by bungee cords that attach to a harness.

"Behind the dining area on your left and right, you'll see individual telephone booth-sized sleeping quarters, each of which provides privacy, a vertical sleeping space, and a porthole through which a crew member can marvel at this world and beyond. The third sleeping compartment is back in the US laboratory but lacks its own window.

"So, Chris, as you see, the living area in the space station comes at a real premium because it costs $5,000 to $10,000 per pound to launch into orbit. As a result, the customary rectangular expanses of a home—a bedroom, kitchen, and living room—have been condensed and occupy the areas adjacent to the aft corridor. Hopefully the view makes up for it. That concludes the grand tour."

Brian glides over to the blood-red crew table and motions everyone else to join him. Shortly the rest of the crew members do so.

"Leslie and Nikolai will join us in a few minutes," Brian says.

"Good," Susan says, still looking around the module's interior. "It's quite a place you have here."

"Yes," Brian says, "it would be quite a real estate listing. Sleep-in closets, short commute to work, great view—" Suddenly Chris feels a jolt followed immediately by the sound of a klaxon.

Fear races through Chris in an instant.

"That's the electrical alarm!" Brian exclaims. "But we have power here. We must be running on batteries." Rapidly the rest of the crew members scatter as Brian and Susan hastily make their way forward to the bank of laptops, which practically guards the forward hatch opening. Looking at one of the laptop's screens, Brian announces, "The starboard P-6 solar arrays have been damaged, and the remote power control modules have shut down all power to the port side as well."

After he turns around to face the rest of the crew members, Brian yells over the din, "Sentilles, turn off that alarm! Antipov, take my place and let me know if there are any changes in the status of our electrical problems! Hastings, tell Houston that we have lost power from our P-6 solar arrays." He turns to Susan and barks, "Wells, undock the shuttle and report any signs of damage to the solar arrays and the space station!"

"Yes, sir!" Susan says. She turns around, motions to her crew, and then exclaims, "Howard and Cole, follow me!" Susan floats to the forward hatch opening and disappears through it. Next is Xavier, who zigzags his way to the passageway and squirms through. Finally, Chris takes his turn scrambling forward. Not quite the space acrobat as the others since he's a rookie astronaut, Chris hovers momentarily near the sunken green floor. With adrenaline coursing through his veins, Chris launches himself over the bank of laptop workstations to the forward hatch opening. But in his haste, his ill-judged trajectory is too high—nearly vertical. To his horror, the handholds to the passageway are just beyond his reach! Before Chris has a chance to recover, his head hits the vault-like hatch stowed parallel to and a foot below the ceiling, where the sound of the collision is masked by the alarm.

CHAPTER 3

A CRUCIBLE OF FIRE

Slowly Chris's senses return. But his sense of pain he could do without, for his headache is unrelenting. Along his chest, a familiar pressure restricts his movements. The dissonance gradually modulates into distinct speech over the whir of avionics. And light, shadows, and color eventually morph into objects, though not the ample surroundings of the space station. Slowly he realizes that he is secured to his seat on the space shuttle—the only one without his pressure suit and gloves! Fortunately for him, the flight crew members haven't donned their helmets yet.

The commander and pilot are seated in front of him. Behind him, he hears Brian in the aft flight deck announcing, "Confirm damage to both starboard P-6 solar arrays. Perhaps of greater concern is that the space station is listing about ten degrees to starboard."

"Copy that," Mission Control says. "ISS Mission Commander Sergei Antipov, actuate the remote power control modules through the use of your laptop and restore power to the port side of the P-6 solar arrays. *Endeavor*, Houston, you are cleared to land at Edwards Air Force Base. Go for the deorbit burn in twenty minutes."

"Roger, go for the deorbit burn in twenty minutes," Susan says. "Landing at Edwards Air Force Base." Glancing at Xavier, she adds,

"That doesn't leave us with much time to prepare. We'll be landing at two in the morning."

"What's going on?" Chris mumbles, fighting off his sluggishness.

"We tried to revive you, but we were unable to," Brian says as he floats over to Chris. "The flight surgeon at Mission Control said to bring you back as soon as possible. Then it was the flight director's decision to exchange Expedition crews ahead of schedule. The rest of the departing ISS crew members are seated in the middeck."

"But I didn't have a chance to launch my payload!" Chris growls while he rubs the top of his head with his right hand.

"Sorry, Chris," Brian says, dropping his voice. "You're not in any shape to do that. Unfortunately there wasn't any time to move equipment from the multipurpose logistics module into the space station, so that will have to be done on another mission. In any event, we will deorbit shortly."

"But I'll never have this chance again!" Chris says, bristling with indignation. He pauses for a few moments to collect himself. Looking through the right overhead window and seeing his supposed home inverted above the shuttle, he asks, "By the way, how is the space station?"

"Apparently some space debris damaged the right main solar panels on a large T-like structure," Brian explains. "The electrical system computers sensed this, which forced the station to run on batteries. But don't worry. Everything will be okay. Once we restore electricity from the left main solar arrays shortly, it will be supplemented by power generated from the remaining smaller solar panels on the other modules, which should be sufficient to power the space station."

"All right," Chris says, puzzled and still in pain. "But why are we landing at Edwards Air Force Base? Isn't that in California?"

"Yes, it is," Brian says. "Don't you remember that a tropical disturbance was approaching Kennedy Space Center when we launched?"

"Yes."

"The storm is over our primary landing site right now. But we can't fly through rain because it will damage the shuttle's heat-resistant tiles. So we will have to go to our secondary landing site, which is Edwards Air Force Base. Since we'll be deorbiting soon, it's too late to put on your pressure suit. So hang in there until we land."

"Thanks," Chris grumbles as Brian disappears through the left interdeck opening—a rectangular gap in the floor that's just large enough to let one astronaut at a time float through from one deck to the other.

No! This can't be happening! Chris thinks as the orbiter departs the space station. His heart pounding, his veins bulging from his neck, Chris shakes his head in disbelief as anger flashes in his eyes.

* * *

The commander and pilot quickly ready the shuttle to land. Nearly halfway around the world from the landing site, still upside down and tail first, the spacecraft fires its engines for a little more than three minutes. Having slowed down by 205 miles per hour, a decrease of a mere 1 percent, they begin their descent. Several minutes later, after a series of cannon-like bursts, the orbiter transitions to a traditional nose-first, wings-level position relative to Earth.

The rest of the crew, except for the commander, has little to do except look out a window until landing.

The spacecraft, traveling close to seventeen thousand miles per hour and only thirty minutes away from touchdown, enters

Earth's atmosphere with the nose inclined at a forty-degree angle, and weightlessness ends for the astronauts.

So fast is the shuttle's speed into an ever-denser atmosphere that the air around it ionizes from shockwaves, forming a pink-purple cone of fire that surrounds the orbiter. Periodic bursts of light shine through the overhead windows, which illuminate the commander and pilot's seat backs.

Through a crucible of fire, man and machine descend, leaving a luminescent trail for thousands of miles in their wake.

But the astronauts are unconcerned about the unfolding spectacle, for a modern shield protects the spacecraft from searing plasma gases. Reinforced carbon-carbon, which covers surfaces that receive the most intense heat, insulates the nose cone, the wings' leading edges, and the vertical stabilizer where temperatures can reach more than three thousand degrees. However, because of its heavy weight, the material is used sparingly.

Lining the bottom of the shuttle, bordering the two front cockpit windows, and outlining the control surfaces are black tiles that protect against heat of twenty-three hundred degrees. White tiles, the last major insulating materials, cap the top two thirds of the orbiter, shielding it from temperatures up to twelve hundred degrees.

Soon the ionized air around the spacecraft fades and surrenders to the darkness over the Pacific Ocean. Yet the stellar beacons reign in the sky, still claiming the night.

The ultimate glider, the fleeting delta-winged silhouette swoops over the runway with nary a sound until it lands with a sudden jolt. And with a collective sigh of relief, their mission is over.

After a long absence, that familiar tug of gravity returns.

Earth, which had been rapidly scrolling below them for several hours, is oddly no longer moving beyond the cockpit windows, except for the faint flicker of approaching ground-support vehicles.

* * *

Inside the crew transport vehicle, NASA's version of a mobile lounge used at Dulles International Airport to shuttle passengers to and from remote aircraft, the rest of the crew members except Chris finish changing into their dark blue jumpsuits that are adorned with various patches along their shoulders and chests.

A spectacled woman, clad in a white lab coat and crowned with flaxen hair that's swept back into a bun, strides into the cabin. Addressing the injured astronaut, she says, "Hi, Chris. My name is Dr. Trimball. I was told that you needed medical attention."

"Yes, but I really needed some medical attention *up there!*" Chris says, pointing upward and still bitter. "Now I have lost my chance to deploy my experiment on this mission, and if I'm really lucky, I'll have another chance to do so in a few years."

"I'm sorry to hear about that, Chris," Dr. Trimball says, "but that's not my concern. Now, where's your injury?"

"I misjudged my way floating over to a hatch opening," Chris explains, "banged my head against the hatch, and was knocked unconscious."

"All right," Dr. Trimball says. She takes a step closer. "Let me take a look at you." She removes a penlight instrument from her breast pocket, turns it on, and holds it close to Chris's right eye for a few seconds. Then she repeats the process on Chris's left orb. Finally she steps back and asks, "How many fingers am I holding up?"

"Two," Chris says.

"Good. That's all that I can do here." Turning to Susan, Dr. Trimball advises, "Chris will need further tests at the hospital. We'll need to leave as soon as possible."

* * *

As their car pulls up to the emergency entrance, Dr. Trimball tells the driver, "Thanks for the ride." The doctor and her patient get out of the vehicle. They amble from the curb to the double-glass sliding doors and enter the hospital, where they proceed along a florescent-lit hallway and disappear into Dr. Trimball's examination room.

Hours pass. The pace ebbs. And sleep endures—except for newly admitted patients and their caregivers.

Many tests and examinations later, a bored Chris—now wearing a white polo shirt, blue jeans, and sneakers—leaves Dr. Trimball's office. He rolls his black suitcase behind him along the hallway and approaches two people sitting in the waiting room. As Chris draws closer, two strangers immediately spot him and stand up. The taller man with a full head of silvery hair and attired in a pressed white shirt with gray slacks intercepts Chris. "Excuse me," the stranger says. "Are you Chris Cole?"

"Yes," Chris says, wondering whether a bad day is about to get worse. "Why?"

"I'm Michael Sullivan, and this is Andrew Moran," the stranger says. Chris shakes their hands.

His dark hair crew cut, his face weathered, and his torso lean and trim, Andrew wears khaki pants and a burgundy-striped, long-sleeved dress shirt. In a baritone and authoritative voice he says, "I heard that an astronaut was injured, so I came here. What happened?"

"I banged my head against the hatch in my haste to get from one module to the next during an emergency," Chris says as he stands his roller suitcase upright and then rubs the top of his head. "So I traveled all the way to the space station, and all I got was this bump on my head."

"That's not such a good souvenir," Michael says, who then glances at Andrew.

"But the doctor examined and released me from the hospital," Chris says in astonishment.

"I'm glad to see that you're okay," Michael says with earnestness.

"Me too!" Andrew chimes in.

"You were behind closed doors for a long time," Michael says. "What was going on?"

"I'm happy that you're here," Chris says, his eyes flicking between the two strangers, "but I'm not quite sure why you're asking me about my stay here."

"Oh, I'm an electrical engineer who works for the company that built the solar arrays for the space station," Michael says. "It was big news when the ISS was struck by a micrometeor—space debris probably from a launched satellite—and damaged its two main right-side solar arrays. My beeper went off in the middle of the night, and my manager told me to come here as soon as possible."

"I suspected that was the cause of damage," Chris says. "I was told that the remaining solar panels should provide sufficient power."

"That is correct," Michael says.

Nodding, Chris asks, "What about the shuttle's flight crew?"

"They're on a conference call being debriefed by the flight director," Michael says.

"I'd imagine that NASA still needs your services right now," Chris ventures.

"Andrew and I talked to the flight director on the phone very early this morning to assist with the damage assessment," Michael explains. "But they don't need us for the time being."

"I see," Chris says. Turning to Andrew, Chris asks, "And what do you do?"

"I'm a retired astronaut who was part of the Expedition 1 crew back in 2001."

"Wow, that must have been exciting."

Andrew looks away and says wistfully, "Exciting and yet sad because my mother died during my mission."

"I'm so sorry," Chris says, expressing his condolences.

"Thank you. That was many years ago." Looking at Chris again, Andrew adds in an upbeat tone, "Just as my fellow astronauts helped me in my time of need, I'm here to help you."

"That's mighty kind of you," Chris says.

"Thank you," Andrew says. "Regarding the space station, on my last mission it was quite small then. But it's been growing ever since."

"How long were you up there?"

"About four months."

Looking askance at Andrew, Chris says, "I was in space less than a day."

"Sorry to hear about that," Andrew says, "but at least you're okay."

"Thanks," Chris says, looking at Andrew again and nodding subtly. Satisfied with the strangers' explanations, Chris says, "Earlier this morning the doctor asked me some questions like, 'What's your name?' 'Where are you?' 'Do you feel nauseous?' Then she gave me a CT scan, read the radiologist's report, and here I am."

"Looking on the bright side," Andrew says, "at least you have been discharged."

"Yes," Chris says, "and I never thought I'd have a welcoming party."

"Since your mission was cut short, what might cheer you up is attending a medieval fair with me in Big Bear today," Andrew suggests, extending an open hand toward Chris. "I used to have a second home there, and I still follow what goes on in the area since the town's airport isn't far away. I had originally planned to go, but this emergency came along. Do the two of you have the rest of the day free?"

"No, I need to stay here in case NASA has any more questions about the electrical system," Michael says, pointing to his laptop on the chair.

"That's too bad," Andrew says. Turning to Chris, Andrew asks, "How about you?"

Chris weighs his options as he draws his hand to his chin, wondering whether his presence is required for the rest of the day at the base. "Where's Big Bear?" he asks.

"The town is approximately a hundred miles northeast of Los Angeles," Andrew says, "and seventy-five miles southeast of here. It will only take us about forty minutes to get there in my plane."

"I definitely need some fun today to keep me from dwelling on the largest setback of my career," Chris says. "Anyway, I'll need to check in with Kennedy Space Center first." Chris steps away from the group, retrieves his cell phone from his belt holster, dials the number, and says, "Hi, Ms. Torres, this is Chris Cole."

"Hi, Chris," Ms. Torres says. "Sorry about the mishap, but I'm glad you're okay! You are scheduled to fly back from Edwards Air Force Base to Kennedy Space Center on a Gulfstream IV that will be leaving at 2:00 p.m. tomorrow. So be ready to board your plane fifteen minutes beforehand."

"Okay. Where will I be staying?"

"We're still working on that. What can I say? Your arrival at Edwards caught us by surprise. We'll find out later this afternoon and let you know. Anyway, don't forget to bring your flight crew ID with you tomorrow."

"Don't worry. I won't forget it, and I'll look forward to your call later on today about my lodging arrangements. Good-bye," he adds as he ends the call.

"My flight leaves tomorrow afternoon," Chris says as he returns to the group. "So I'll be able to attend the fair and then return with you here later on today or tonight."

"Great," Andrew says. "Let's get going."

CHAPTER 4

THE DAWN OF A NEW DAY

Andrew's light, twin-engine aircraft, a Beechcraft Baron, bolts down the runway and climbs above the horizon.

"Not as exciting as the shuttle, is it?" Chris muses on his headset.

"No," Andrew says, "but I can land my plane in a lot more places."

As their airplane climbs higher into the sky, the sun peeks above the eastern horizon to greet them. Soon the haze that had shrouded the ground burns off and reveals a hardscrabble terrain. To the west, the cotton wisps of change obscure the horizon.

The sight of migrating birds breaks up the tedium of the flight.

In the distance the rugged San Bernardino Mountains, bathed in the soft yellow light of morning, emerge on the horizon. Yet, it doesn't take long for the airplane to reach them. Rising up from the desert floor, eight-thousand-foot peaks pass beneath the aircraft. A veritable oasis in Southern California, a region well-known for its thirst and extended grasp of water, this mountainous area, through orographic lift, wrings any moisture left from the air leaving the Los Angeles basin.

Tucked in the mountains is a blue sliver of water eight miles long by one mile wide with a dam on its western edge and an airport on its eastern margin. Below them, a lone sailboat plies the lake's serene waters. Scattered marinas hem the shore, and nearby hamlets peep from a blanket of trees.

Andrew reduces power and lowers the flaps. His aircraft lands a few minutes afterward.

* * *

As the two of them approach the fair, castle walls interspersed with a series of flanking towers upon which brightly colored flags wave mark the fair's northern boundary. Behind the imposing barrier clamors various wandering acts over the hubbub of large crowds. Andrew and Chris pay their admission fee and then join the horde streaming into the fair, where the latter notices that the two of them seem to be the only ones in modern-day dress. In fact, their fellow visitors are draped in fabrics steeped in cornflower blue, deep carrot orange, puce, and magnolia. Apparently his fellow guests take their visits a lot more seriously than the two of them, Chris surmises.

Underneath the arboreal shade of towering oak, aspen, and pine trees, their musk permeating the air, cheerful shops dot the land. On their left, they pass a troupe entertaining a throng of visitors. Farther up the road a sole piper, lost among the multitudes, pipes above the din.

Chris plots his next move as the two of them approach a large map suspended by two wooden poles.

While he is standing at the fair entrance that corresponds to the map's northeast section, Chris eyes areas of interest. Ye Olde Artisans occupies the northwest region. Fun, Food & Drink sits in the southwest corner. Town Centre stands in the middle of the premises. The Combat Arena resides halfway along the southern boundary. The King's Court lies in the southeast area, and the Globe Theatre is located midway along the eastern edge.

Taking a step closer, Chris points to a spot about halfway along the map's right margin, looks at Andrew, and asks, "How about the Globe Theater since it's the closest to us?"

Andrew purses his lips for a few moments and then says, "Yeah, let's go there."

They follow the lane that winds to their left and then skirts the empty Globe Theatre on their right whose sign reads, "Shows at 10:00, 11:00, 2:00, 3:00, and 4:00."

"I guess we'll have to come back later," Andrew says, looking at his watch. "The first show is forty-five minutes from now."

"All right," Chris says impatiently. "Let's keep going."

To his delight, music erupts farther up the lane. Soon several minstrels skip and caper past them, sowing high spirits in their wake.

As the grade steepens, the road narrows and meanders through the woods. The two of them enjoy the cool shade of summer, verdant canopies, and a chorus of birds until they emerge from the forest, squinting. To their left, a modest retaining wall, which diminishes farther up the lane, limits their view. Before long the two approach a sign where three paths converge—on their left the way to the King's Court, on their right the lane to the Combat Arena, and diagonally on their right, almost backtracking, the route to Town Centre.

"How about the King's Court?" Andrew asks.

"Might as well," Chris huffs. "I don't want to hike back there again."

They head that way, which delivers them to a wide, grassy field where a gathering crowd piques their interest. On the crest of an adjacent hill looms a modest stone castle that rules the countryside.

"It looks like something is about to start," Chris ventures, anxious to attend the day's first event.

"Let's go!" Andrew says, and they both scramble northward toward the multitudes, which, as the two draw closer, are gathered around a nearby stage. Not content to stand at the back of the audience, they press their way to the front of the crowd.

Before them is a breathtaking view of Big Bear Lake framed by gently sloping mountains in the background and a stage in the foreground flanked by three-story castle towers from which trumpeters announce the royal couple's arrival. With regal splendor, the king and queen lead the procession up the stairs and across the middle of the stage followed by the rest of the ranks of the English nobility, who eventually seat themselves behind the royal couple.

When silence reigns, the monarch, topped by a foliated gold crown, graced with a trimmed beard, flecked with gray hair, and bedecked in a red velvet cloak, advances to the front of the platform. The stout sovereign declares in an English accent, "My loyal subjects, through my munificence, it pleases me to see all of you here on the last day of the festival. As is customary each year to celebrate the occasion, I hold a tournament to see who here has the fortitude, agility, cunning, and valor to become a knight, which, as you know, is ordinarily unobtainable through your meager means. The winner will be able to forge a new destiny! Glory, adventure, and conquest are yours if you win! You will have until the end of the day to hone your skills. Since there is only a short time to allow for training and to conduct the contest, I will be limiting the tournament to four people, and thus there will be only two rounds."

Cheers ring out from the audience. The crown continues, "As demonstrated by our victory at the Battle of Crécy and later at the Battle of Poitiers, French mounted knights, who were previously invincible against our foot soldiers, suffered tremendous casualties

29

against an onslaught of our longbows. Since we expect the French to adopt our tactics at the next outbreak of hostilities, it is imperative that our knights be as good or better on foot than on their steeds. As a result, today's contest will be confined to fighting without the aid of horses."

Gasps spring from the audience.

"Contenders who fall, drop, or become separated from their weapon or become too fatigued during battle lose. The victor of the tournament will be knighted late this afternoon, which will be followed shortly thereafter by a parade here at the King's Court to celebrate the occasion." Applause greets the king.

"Who here would like to be the first challenger?" the monarch asks, motioning with his right hand from one side of the audience to the other. A stampede rushes forward, carrying Chris and Andrew along with them to the front of the stage. Immediately a sea of hands sprouts from the crowd.

The sovereign walks a few steps to his left and apparently selects the tallest person he can find. "You there!" the crown bellows. "The tall one carrying an axe. You are the first competitor!"

Selected, the goateed and grinning man, whose sinewy physique looms at least a head length above the others and whose dark mane flows over his shoulders, turns and faces the crowd as the audience cheers. After the contestant raises his hand to acknowledge the crowd, a diagonal scar across his right forearm becomes apparent, which Chris imagines to be a badge of a previous violent encounter.

"Probably the local enforcer," Chris jokes.

Andrew nods.

"Who else would like to join the contest?" the king asks. A few anxious moments later he points to Chris's left and says, "Yes, you over there with the shaved head." Someone who could easily pass as a dungeon master—a stocky, petulant man whose wrinkles seem to have permanently etched his countenance in a sullen mood—manages but a quick smile before he returns to his natural state as the audience applauds.

"Are there any other worthy contenders gathered here?" the monarch asks, gesturing to the horde. "You there—the man with filthy red hair and grimy white tunic near the front of the crowd," the sovereign announces, pointing to the individual. Chris turns his head and spots an intrepid figure with a narrow face, exuding the ardor of youth. Claps reign from the gallery.

"Must be a laborer," Chris says softly.

"Probably," Andrew says.

Again the hands rise eagerly, but the crown raises his hand to quell the clamoring throng, which quickly becomes silent. "Let it be said that I am just in selecting challengers," the king says. "Unlike past years in which I selected the strongest and most fearless competitors, this year I will seek a representative of you—someone of *average* bearing and ability. No need to raise your hand. I will choose the last person." Slowly the monarch walks across the stage, surveying his minions while the stunned audience murmurs softly. He approaches Chris, points at him, and declares, "This man here will be the last contender. Those strange raiments won't hide the fact that somewhere in that slight build of yours, ambition to become mightier and stronger died a long time ago. Let's see if the opportunity to become a knight rekindles your resolve—a chance to change your fortune forever!"

From the crowd, cheers swell and eventually ebb.

"Today," the sovereign continues, "the four of you will be engaged in a severe test, and as recompense, each of you will have lunch with the royal family in the castle at one o'clock." The audience cheers briefly. "The tournament will be held at the Combat Arena, which is off to your left, a minute's walk from here," the crown adds, extending his right hand. "Those chosen by me are invited to participate in the contest that will begin at four o'clock."

Signaling the king's departure, the royal trumpets play again.

"You there in the odd clothes!" a voice calls out. Andrew and Chris turn to their right and see one of the king's acolytes hurrying toward them. Stopping in front of Chris, the attendant, who is slightly out of breath, thrusts a missive into Chris's hand and declares, "Since you are one of the challengers in today's tournament, it would please His Majesty if you could use his decree to purchase armor of your liking at any blacksmith shop. Now if you'll excuse me, I need to find the rest of the competitors. Good luck!" he cries and then disappears into a sea of visitors.

As the crowd disperses, Andrew, who looks distantly at the stage, says, "You'll be busy for the rest of today."

"I'm just as surprised as you are," Chris says. "It isn't all bad news. Let's see if I can improve physically. But it doesn't matter if I fail to advance to the second round."

"Most of the day will be over by then," Andrew says, placing his hands on his hips, looking at Chris again.

"I don't want to disappoint the king," Chris says as he thrusts the letter into his pocket. "Hopefully I won't let you and the spectators down either."

As the two retrace their steps across the field, Andrew asks, "When and where do you want to meet next?"

"Why don't we meet at the Combat Arena around four fifteen?" Chris asks. "If I don't win the first round, we can leave earlier than we planned to."

"How about before lunch?" Andrew suggests. A look of disappointment crawls across his face. "Who knows, you could have changed your mind by then."

Mindful of not wanting to offend his only ride back to base, Chris says reluctantly, "Just call me on my cell phone because I have no idea where I'm going to be at any given time except for lunch."

"Okay, then I'll give you a call later on today."

* * *

Along the lane whose sign reads, "Town Centre," Chris ventures into the forest until it surrenders to a clearing. A cluster of small quaint buildings surrounds a circular path that rings a three-story lookout tower. *Certainly I should find a map of the fair here*, Chris thinks, hopeful to locate the appropriate person who could begin his training soon.

Starting at the southeast entrance of the rotary, he advances counterclockwise, passing a souvenir shop, and just beyond it there's a lane heading to the northeast marked, "Faire Exit." Pressing on, he travels by a theater followed by a road extending to the northwest whose sign reads, "Ye Olde Artisans." Chris winds his way past a privies building and a path bearing to the west marked, "Fun, Food & Drink." Then farther still, he comes upon a first-aid booth, another lane with the same sign as the last ascending toward the southwest, and a food court. Finally he reaches his starting point— the route leading to the southeast whose sign reads, "King's Court and Combat Arena."

Frustrated, Chris strolls into the first floor of the lookout tower and enters a tavern, much to his amazement. He walks over to the barkeeper, who is drying off spirit glasses, and asks, "Do you know where I could find a map of this place?"

"Sorry, we're out of maps," the barkeeper says, "but this is the last day of the fair. Don't worry. Just follow the signs."

Flustered, Chris marches out the door and wonders with growing concern. *How am I going to get started if I can't find a map? I don't want to drag my feet back to the fair entrance, where Andrew and I last saw one. Where am I going to find help? I could really use a map right now.* Guessing that a blacksmith plies his trade at Ye Olde Artisans and that he might know someone who could train him, Chris heads in that direction.

Abruptly from behind him a blur of feathers sweeps past, gliding along a wide arc until it nears its master sitting on a chestnut horse standing on the crest of a distant bridge. The bird of prey flutters until it alights on his master's outstretched gloved hand, shrieking.

Chris pauses to gather his wits, his heart racing from the surprise. With a sigh, he resumes his journey and eventually joins the trio.

Hooded, svelte, and pint-sized, the slate-gray raptor perches atop its master's hand. The winged beast is secured by short leather straps attached to its legs.

"That's quite a bird you have there," Chris says. "Is that a falcon?"

"Indeed it is," the goateed falconer says in an English tone. Emblazoned in a parti-colored scarlet-and-gold doublet, he looks down at Chris and says, "It's a peregrine falcon."

"It certainly looks fearsome," Chris observes. "If your falcon got any bigger, I'd bet it would attack us."

"You're probably right," the falconer says.

"By the way, do you know where I can find a map?" Chris asks, switching to a more pressing subject.

"There's a large one near the fair entrance," the falconer says. "Why do you ask?"

"I just entered a tournament whose winner will be knighted," Chris says, "and I was trying to find someone who could teach me how to use a sword. Would you know of anyone?"

"Well, it has been awhile," the falconer says, looking away and sighing. After lolling his head slightly from left to right, he adds, "I know someone who can help you. Follow me!"

Surprisingly the falconer leads Chris back to Town Centre, away from Ye Olde Artisans—the most likely location in which to find a blacksmith who might know an expert swordsman, Chris assumes.

"Hey, aren't we going the wrong way if we want to meet someone who can train me?" Chris asks.

"Don't worry," the falconer says. "I know my way around these parts."

Frustrated, Chris tags along on foot, wondering whether he's made a mistake.

The two wend their way around the lookout tower and then travel along the road marked, "Fun, Food & Drink." For a short while, they plod westward up a long ascending path that switches back in the opposite direction.

"Why have the fair on such hilly terrain?" Chris asks, tired of such undulations. "It was such an effort to get to the King's Court earlier today. I'm getting worn out just walking."

"Typically that's the hallmark of castle locations," the falconer says. "Besides, your effort today will result in greater stamina tomorrow."

"But it's today I'm worried about," Chris says.

"Hang in there," the falconer says. "It's not much farther."

At the top of a hill they approach two prominent buildings, beyond which the faint jangle of distant crowds emanates. The air grows redolent of savory meats, potatoes, and onions. On their left a whole hog is slowly being rotated, roasting over an open fire. On their right, between the assorted food shops and spirits stands, ensconced in the first and second buildings, gapes a wide entrance to a courtyard teeming with people.

After they pass the enclosure, they draw up to the next building, whose last shop sign on their right reads, "Bacchus Wines."

"Can you do me a favor and have the proprietor meet me outside because I don't want to dismount and walk around with my raptor perched on my hand?" the falconer asks.

"Sure," Chris says, who subsequently disappears inside the store.

A few minutes later Chris returns outside with the merchant in tow.

"Good man," the falconer says, "my acquaintance is in need of training for today's contest, whose champion will be knighted. Can the wizard help him?"

"Give me a minute to see if he's agreeable to the idea," the tradesman says in an English dialect and then disappears inside his shop.

An expression of frustration creeps across the falconer's face. "That's odd," the man on horseback says. "I don't remember the wizard being that busy the last time I was here."

"What do you have to do to prepare for the tournament around here?" Chris wonders aloud, disheartened.

Five agonizing minutes pass until the proprietor reappears outside his shop and motions Chris to come inside.

"Good luck, young man!" the falconer says.

"Thanks for all your help!" Chris says. He follows the merchant inside the shop, and they eventually stop at a back door, whereupon the tradesman gestures to the portal.

Chris's eyes narrow on an odd black metal door, which has several horizontal gaps near the bottom that must presumably function as a vent. He opens the door and ventures in. Abruptly the portal behind him slams shut, plunging him into darkness with the exception of a flickering light at the end of the corridor. His footsteps echoing off the walls, his body brushed by a draft, Chris slowly advances toward the dancing yellow lights on the far wall and enters a small chamber on his right with a stone-filled floor and cobweb-draped walls. Standing in front of and silhouetted against a hearth with a small crackling fire is the wizard, who appears to be reading a book on a lectern, casting a larger-than-life shadow on the opposite wall.

Hesitantly Chris advances into the firelight. In one corner he hears a fly trying to escape. In another he sees a snake slowly slithering away.

"Excuse me," Chris says, mustering some courage and interrupting the hiss of the fire. "You're a wizard, aren't you?"

The sage, whose head pivots up to meet Chris's gaze, says in a low and distinguished English timbre, "Yes, most people call me that, and some call me by other names. What brings you here?"

"The king selected me to be in a tournament whose winner will be knighted," Chris says, standing rigidly. "Can you help me?"

"Give my regards to the king when you see him," the wizard says distantly.

"How can I give myself a chance to win then?" Chris asks.

The wizard hesitates and then growls, "I spend my time with kings. In the great events of the world—epic battles, power, avarice, and treachery—*you* need some help learning how to wield a sword. Look at you. You don't even have one, and you don't talk like a monarch either."

"The falconer sounded pretty sure that you could help me," Chris says with a rising lump in his throat.

"If you are not a king," the wizard rumbles, "then you have no kingdom!"

Chris collects his thoughts, realizes that his current approach is doomed to failure, and tries a different tact. "It's not a kingdom in the traditional sense," he says.

"It's a simple yes or no question," the wizard says, his voice dripping with sarcasm.

"I am not so much trying to save anyone's kingdom," Chris says, sidestepping the query. "Rather, I am trying to improve my own."

The wizard slowly taps his spindly fingers against the lectern.

"I tend to think of a kingdom as my domain and what I am able to accomplish within it," Chris says, wringing his hands, "which has been lacking for quite some time."

The wizard's silence enhances the hiss and crackle of the fire behind him. His fingers now motionless, the sage looks down at his book and says, "I am sorry. I cannot help you prepare for the tournament."

Demoralized, Chris slumps forward slightly and lets out a sigh.

"But I know someone *else* who can," the wizard says.

"Thank you so much!" Chris exclaims, happy that his quest to find an instructor appears to be over. "Science has dominated my life for so long … at the expense of my body. I've tried to get physically fit for the longest time, but I just can't find a way."

"You were fortunate to mention *kingdom*," the wizard says.

"Why do you say that?" Chris asks.

"Because," the wizard says, "a good mind possesses a kingdom."[1] Shrugging, he adds, "Otherwise I'm not sure I would have offered to help you."

"I had no idea," Chris says, glad that something in his conversation changed the sage's mind.

"You have much conviction in your quest for help," the wizard says, apparently stroking his beard in silhouette. "That's good. But it's unfortunate that your kingdom lies dormant while others prosper."

"Then how do I expand mine?" Chris asks.

"The day is young," the wizard says. "You can't learn everything in an instant. In any event, I am glad you volunteered. Rarely outside of your craft do you get called upon to improve yourself. You would think people would wait until they were struck by lightning, have the earth tremble beneath them, witness the immense power of a volcanic eruption, or hear God say, 'Get cracking!' before lifting a finger. You toil in your trade for untold hours every day, but how much time do you dedicate outside your handicraft to become a stronger, wiser, and more persevering individual? Perhaps you will be a changed man after all this."

"I'm looking forward to that," Chris says, shifting his stance uneasily. Eager to get on with it, he adds, "Look, I'm sure you're busy and you've got better things to do. Perhaps you can tell me your friend's name and where his shop is, and then I will find him on my own."

"I don't think he would help strangers if they just came in off the street," the wizard says. "In fact, anyone can say that they are a friend of mine regardless of whether it is so. And even if it were the case, you can't expect to meet complete strangers and have them do favors for you."

"I can pay him," Chris says.

"I don't care how much gold you have!" the wizard snaps, shaking his head slowly. "My friend only teaches whenever he feels like it, and if we go over there and meet him, I think he will help you."

"Great," Chris says, happy with any positive outcome.

"So why were you chosen?" the sage inquires. "You don't seem to be the type."

"He thought I was average," Chris says, swallowing his pride, "and that I represented the common man."

"Forget what the king thinks. Noble by birth, he knows no other life. Were it not for his lineage, he would have no doubt started as a lowly soldier. Perhaps injury or death would have cut short his climb through the ranks."

Chris nods.

"Anyway, I'm glad he chose you because now you have a chance to achieve great things," the wizard says. "Be not afraid of greatness: some are born great, some achieve greatness, and some have greatness thrust upon them."[2]

"Greatness?" Chris echoes, his spirits rising, though unsure how that term applies to him.

"This is a defining point in your life," the wizard says, leaning toward Chris. "But you are not alone in your quest, for you have my help as well as my friend's."

"How are the other competitors going to prepare for today's contest?" Chris asks, looking ahead to his first-round match.

"Some will rely on natural ability," the wizard explains, "and others will seek out experts who will be able to help them."

"That doesn't sound fair," Chris says.

"What makes you think that life is fair?" the wizard rumbles.

"Okay, let's go see your friend," Chris says, beckoning to the corridor.

"Not so fast!" the wizard cautions. "My friend only instructs people who have overcome at least one of their fears recently."

"You're kidding," Chris says as fissures spread over his brow. "Why would your friend make such a request?"

"That's what you need to do if you want his help," the wizard says. "He has not learned the lesson of life who does not every day surmount a fear."[3]

"That's a tall order."

"Have you done that?"

"No," Chris says, annoyed that anyone would have the time to do any such thing.

"Have you conquered any fear over the last twenty years?" the wizard asks.

"No," Chris says again sheepishly.

"Why haven't you done anything?" the wizard asks, his voice rising in frustration.

"If I didn't try it," Chris says, "I wouldn't be disappointed."

"Don't you realize that you are locking yourself in a dungeon of your own making?" the wizard asks, raising his right hand in silhouette. "The cautious seldom err."[4]

"But I didn't lose."

"And you didn't win either."

"Is it not enough that I battle foes today," Chris asks, his body stiffening against the verbal onslaught, "but I must also conquer myself?"

"That would be a good start since you wish to change yourself," the wizard advises the swordsman-to-be. "Far better it is to dare mighty things, to win glorious triumphs, even though checkered by failure, than to take rank with those poor spirits who neither enjoy much nor suffer much, because they live in the gray twilight that knows not victory nor defeat."[5]

"That's easy for you to say," Chris says, taking offense. "You're a wizard. You just wave your staff, and things have a way of working out."

"Don't change the subject!" the wizard admonishes. "I'm not the person seeking change. You are. Without conquering a fear, you cannot move forward. In fact, you could say you're moving backward slowly."

"How is that?"

"Iron rusts from disuse; stagnant water loses its purity and in cold weather becomes frozen; even so does inaction sap the vigor of the mind."[6]

"All right," Chris says, warming up to the idea. "I'll resolve to always move forward then."

"That's very noble of you," the wizard says with a belly laugh.

"Why do you doubt me?" Chris asks, bewildered at the thought.

"Many receive advice, few profit by it,"[7] the wizard says, "which leads back to my question. What fear will you overcome today?"

"Well ... I hate speaking to the public," Chris says, tightening his throat.

"Let me see if I understand you correctly," the wizard intones. "You lack courage, and yet you want to be a knight?"

"It's different!" Chris says.

"Why are you afraid?" the wizard asks, his silhouetted arms outstretched.

"I haven't done this before," Chris says. "I'm a research person. I'm used to conducting experiments by myself, not getting up in front of a lot of people. I present my ideas on a one-on-one basis. So I'm no different from anyone else."

"You are no different from anyone else," the wizard echoes, "in that you have challenges in life. And how you face those challenges will shape your future." The fireplace pops, interrupting him momentarily. "Circumstances rule men; men do not rule circumstances."[8]

"I still get nervous. That's my reality."

"In time, I expect your reality to change. In any event, what kind of experiments did you conduct?"

"Oh, designing various devices to monitor a spacecraft," Chris says, motioning skyward.

"You mean you were in the heavens?" the wizard asks, his silhouetted hand pointing upward.

"Yes, I was up there," Chris says, choosing his words carefully. "My trip was more thrilling than terrifying—or as you put it, 'overcoming a fear.'"

"If you were in the heavens," the wizard inquires sternly, "then why do you need my assistance?"

"A machine with the help of thousands of support people, not to mention the flight crew, launched me into orbit," Chris says with embarrassment. "So I wasn't able to do it all by myself. For the upcoming tournament, I have only myself to rely on."

"You are forgetting that you will have my help and an expert's advice before you battle your foes," the wizard says, correcting him.

Chris nods.

"Now, back to overcoming your fear of speaking to the crowd," the wizard says with renewed vigor, "I still don't understand what is so difficult about talking to a bunch of people."

"Everyone is looking at me," Chris says, his eyes darting from side to side.

"It sounds like someone has cast a spell on you," the wizard says impassively. "Here you are, far away from home, and yet you still don't consider conquering new ground." He pauses for a moment, looks at the ceiling as if expecting to see God, and mutters, "They change their clime, not their disposition, who run across the sea."[9] Looking at Chris again, the wizards asks, "Are you afraid of something new?"

"No," Chris says. "I'm afraid of looking like a fool."

"Where have I heard that before?" the wizard snorts, tinged with sarcasm. "Don't you find it strange that man's sustenance—the social interaction of others—rapidly transmutes into man's greatest woe, with the simple addition of a few extra pair of eyes gazing upon the speaker, unnerving him. It's as if there were a supernatural divide, a chasm, or an invisible gauntlet between those who dare to

seek the stage and those who cower at the possibility of doing so. Those who fear it let their imaginations run wild. What these souls don't know is that speaking to the multitude is not much different from everyday conversation. Fortunately there are those who have overcome their self-doubts."

"Yes, the king and most likely any entertainer," Chris says with a nod. "That's it. Just two types of people."

"You need not be a sovereign or an entertainer to appreciate what influencing the crowd can do for you," the wizard says. "Excel at this endeavor, which people happen to fear more than *death*, and you will find that your fortune will change dramatically. It's like magic! Get used to being the center of attention. Those skills can help you summon the courage to sway your audience, improve your lot in life, and become a leader of men. That's why you should pursue the craft. Who else besides the king caught your attention with a speech?"

"No one," Chris says with a whiff of discontent.

"Then I will use him as an example of *how* to give one."

"All right."

"Did he lock both hands like a fig leaf in front of himself during his address?"

"No."

"Did he only look at and speak to one part of the crowd?" the wizard asks, motioning to his right.

"No."

"How did he learn the craft?"

"I don't know."

"The answer is practice."

"That's the part I am worried about—looking like a fool!" Chris says, exasperated.

"Low are the people who speak ill of others," the wizard says. "Don't worry. You are not a fool. We already have one, and his name is the jester!"

Without warning, the fireplace erupts, expelling glowing embers onto the floor.

"All right," Chris concedes, looking down and extinguishing them with the soles of his sneakers. "I won't let looking like a fool stop me anymore."

"Indeed. To make sure that you overcome this fear of yours," the wizard says, using his silhouetted forefinger to point toward the portal diagonally behind him, "I want you to go outside to the courtyard through this door here and regale the crowd with something memorable that happened to you."

"I have been in space recently," Chris says.

"So you told me," the wizard says mockingly.

"Really, I've been there," Chris says, "but I don't have anything on me to prove it. All my possessions are back where I landed."

Shaking his head, the wizard says, "It doesn't really matter. Your subject won't be relevant here."

"You're right," Chris says, disheartened.

"What other story could you amuse them with?" the wizard asks. "A personal experience? A hobby? A sojourn?"

"Let's see," Chris says, thinking out loud. "I can't talk about work. I can't talk about where I live because no Europeans lived in North America during the Middle Ages." He pauses as the possibilities roll through his head. "I think I'll talk about something that happened to me when I was young."

"Good," the wizard says, pointing at the door once more. "Now go outside and face your fears."

CHAPTER 5

ALL THE WORLD'S A STAGE

Chris opens the back door and is immediately blinded by daylight. The infectious merriment of a piper, the mystical resonance of mandolins and tambourines, and the upbeat tone of drums fill the air with joy. Slowly his vision returns as he staggers away from the harsh glare of the morning sun.

To his delight, Chris joins the same crowd that he had passed several minutes earlier in the courtyard, formed by two long buildings along its northern edge and bordered by castle walls on its remaining sides.

Eager to secure a good perch from which to give a speech, he surveys the quadrangle, gradually rotating his body to follow his turning head. He makes almost a complete turn when he spots his quarry. A ten-foot-high wooden platform, which peeps above the heads of his fellow visitors, is propitiously vacant in front of the eastern wall.

Chris takes a step in that direction and then halts. Doubt ignites fear. *What if no one stops to listen to my speech?* he wonders. *What if I forget what to say when I get up there? What if the audience becomes bored listening to my story and decides to leave? I don't have to give a speech, but then I would have to start over again and find someone else to teach me how to fight with a sword. So telling my story now would be the easier thing to do. Besides, giving a speech shouldn't be tougher than battling foes.*

With that thought, he ambles toward the stand, adjusting his course many times to accommodate the movements of his fellow visitors until he stops in front of an unlikely sentinel—a portly old man attired in a greenish-blue, short-sleeved, knee-length tunic. He sports a forked gray beard, and he is crowned with a wreath of matching hair.

Mustering some courage, Chris strolls up to the fellow and introduces himself, saying, "Hi, I'm Chris."

"James," the stranger responds in kind.

"Glad to meet you," Chris says, firmly shaking James's hand. "I need to give a speech right now, and this appears to be the best spot. Can I do so from here?"

James draws his hand to his brow and appears to ponder the thought for a moment. "I think it would be fine," he affirms with a burgeoning Cheshire-cat smile.

"It looked like you weren't quite sure a second ago," Chris says with a quizzical look. "I don't want to step on any toes. Are you sure it's okay?"

"Yes, I am quite sure," James says emphatically. "So, what are you going to talk about?"

"When I was little," Chris says, "my dad took me on a trip to Alaska to watch the auroras."

"Great subject," James says with a look of concern, "but you can't mention Alaska because the state simply did not exist during the Middle Ages."

"I see," Chris says. "Rather than giving specifics like 'I was in Alaska,' I should say, 'I traveled to the Arctic Circle.'"

"Exactly," James says. "How much time do you need?"

"About two minutes."

"Great!" James says. "Oh, and make sure you project. The last thing you want is someone interrupting your tale by yelling, 'I can't hear you!' Any questions?"

"How do I prevent myself from forgetting my entire speech when I'm up there?"

"Don't worry," James says. "Grasp the subject, the words will follow."[10]

"Are you sure?"

"Of course I am," James says, patting Chris on the back. "How can you forget to describe a family trip? In any event, I want you to go up onstage so that people will know that your speech is nigh."

Obliging, Chris climbs up the steps to the platform where any entertainer could easily regale half the people in the courtyard. A small theater resides on his immediate left with a few brave souls entertaining an audience seated on simple wooden benches. Adjacent to the theater lies the alternating colored squares of the Human Chess Arena, and beyond it stands a pub ensconced in the far corner where some of the patrons are undoubtedly enjoying their inward journey in repose.

To his right are two long half-timbered buildings—each of which house several shops above which roof dormers of various sizes and slopes spring—that flank the courtyard entrance. Residing in the closer structure is the juggler and fortune-teller's booths, and off to his immediate right is the door leading to the wizard's chamber. On the far side of the confines stands the second long building that houses many amusement games.

A fire-breather, a juggler, dueling stilt walkers, and roaming minstrels are scattered about the courtyard beyond the assembling crowd. James grabs a large wooden sign marked, "Two minutes," which he holds high in front of the stand. Instantly Chris's heart starts pounding, his focus scattered. A lump in his throat grows inexorably. The presence of many eyes upon him pierces his soul.

Fighting against coalescing demons of his own making, he struggles to reacquire the mental outline of his speech. Out of the corner of his eye he sees James lift a sign that reads, "One minute," and then paces back and forth for a while until he retires it.

James looks up at Chris and says, "Certainly you had a lot of fun on your trip. Focus on sharing that joy with everyone who is listening to your story. Bring smiles to their faces. Remember, you are going to focus on one person in the audience at a time, complete a thought, and then move on to the next person. If you have any trouble giving your speech, just look at me. Now have fun with it!" He turns away and joins the throng.

After composing himself, Chris says, "Ladies and gentlemen … I mean, good lords and ladies," he corrects. Rattled, he looks plaintively at James, who motions reassuringly with his right hand for Chris to continue. Resuming his speech, Chris adds, "When I was a child, I saw something few people see—an image so powerful that it remains as vivid today as it was thirty-five years ago. While most people, if they had time, would journey south to warmer climates, my father and I traveled north to the Arctic Circle and left civilization behind.

"It was early March, and winter still had a firm grip on the land. The forest was blanketed with deep snow, and the scent of pine trees stirred our spirits. Our path led us to a clearing in a valley where we waited for nightfall. Soon the sun sank below the horizon, and we were all alone in the forest. It was eerily silent except for an occasional howl of a wolf in the nearby mountains.

"One drawback to being that far north at night is extremely low temperatures. In fact, it was so cold that our eyes and the bridges of our noses were the only parts exposed to the elements. Fortunately, there was no wind.

"To help us stay warm, we built a fire that sent embers high into the night's sky.

"After we lay down on blankets, I was struck by how incredibly bright the stars were, and I have been drawn to them ever after! An occasional shooting star, nature's exclamation point, would catch my glimpse.

"Slowly, what we had been waiting for appeared—a spectacular aurora electrified the sky. Like a turbulent river that's dyed sea green, the northern lights flowed slowly across the heavens through an invisible and ever-changing riverbed. Occasionally the ghostly stream branched into two or three channels. It contradicted the senses that such a dynamic and fantastic display unfolded in complete silence.

"To our delight, we enjoyed the northern lights for several hours until some clouds completely obscured our view.

"You, too, can behold the auroras. Journey to the Arctic Circle between late February and March to see nature's most exciting displays, and you will remember it for the rest of your life! Thank you."

As the audience applauds, Chris notices that one person isn't happy at all—a jester who's grimacing with his hands on his hips. He's clad in a vertical parti-color scarlet-and-gold tunic with a matching multitailed hat that's festooned with hat bells.

With mixed emotions, Chris descends the stairs.

"Good speech!" a voice calls out. "How well do you think you did?"

Chris looks to his left and sees James near the landing. "I have to go back and see ... uh, my friend who is behind that door there," Chris says, pointing that way and not wanting to delay his training.

"Oh," James says, raising an eyebrow, "I thought you would like some tips on how to improve your speech."

"Let me check with my friend first," Chris says, "and I'll get back to you."

"All right, Chris," James says, who looks dispirited.

With the weight of the world off his shoulders and eager to start his training, Chris hastily heads back to the wizard's chamber and rejoins the man still silhouetted in the fire-lit room.

"What tidings do you have for me?" the wizard asks, looking up at Chris.

"I had a rough start," Chris admits, "but after that it went okay. I still don't like it though."

"So you were uncomfortable, huh?" the wizard asks, his voice colored with innuendo.

"Yes," Chris says, glad to have finished it.

"You've just got a taste of it," the wizard says. "Do you think if you try it once, that you are forever cured of your particular fear?"

"Probably not," Chris ventures.

"Then get back out there and give another speech!" the wizard exclaims, pointing to the portal again.

Complying, Chris retraces his steps through the back door and enters the courtyard. Slowly he walks back to the platform landing and rejoins James.

"Sorry I couldn't commit a few minutes ago," Chris apologizes. "I wasn't quite sure what I was going to be doing next." His eyes narrowing, he asks, "By the way, why are you so interested in helping me with my speech?"

"Let's just say that I miss hearing the roar of the crowd," James says, whose eyes grow distant.

"All right," Chris says, not sure what to make of that comment.

An awkward silence ensues. Finally James asks, "Was this your first speech?"

"Yes, it was," Chris says guardedly. "How did you know?"

"You appeared nervous, but you survived," James says, extending an open hand toward Chris. "In any event, this is what I liked about your speech. You piqued the audience's interest by saying, 'I saw something few people see.' You went on to set the scene—the time, the setting, the weather—and that we shouldn't miss it. You also had good eye contact with the crowd. Should you give another speech, consider moving around the stand. Try to spend an equal part on the left-hand side of the platform as the right. In addition, I'd like to see you use more gestures."

Chris nods.

"Will you be giving another speech shortly?" James asks as wrinkles etch his forehead.

"Yes, how did you guess?"

"I think that stunned look on your face gave it away. So, what's the subject of your next speech?"

"Do you have a trebuchet?" Chris asks.

"Look around you," James suggests, gesturing to the surrounding landscape. "We simply don't have the space to allow for a demonstration. To have a working model that would impress the public, we'd have to cut down some trees, build a cross section of a castle wall, and then have various tradesman build the weapon. Maybe the king would oblige. Or perhaps he'd like us to build one near an enemy's castle so it could be destroyed, expanding the king's domain."

"All right," Chris says, playing along. "The reason I asked is that my next speech is about a trebuchet."

"How fitting for a medieval fair," James says, his eyes aglow with excitement. "What sparked your interest in that?"

"I like engineering challenges," Chris explains. "Historians didn't know what one looked like until an illustration of one was found many years ago, and I have a picture of one in my office."

"I can't wait to hear your speech," James says with brio. "How much time will you need to prepare?"

"About five minutes."

"Okay, let me get that sign."

As Chris climbs up on the platform, James retrieves his signpost and leans it against the front of the platform. He ambles into the courtyard, where he beckons and then actually herds as many people as he can toward Chris. The newly assembled audience is much larger than the first. With a smirk, James returns to the base of the platform and retrieves his sign.

Either James has a hidden agenda, or he really likes his work, Chris reckons.

Near the back edge of the gathering crowd is the jester who brings giggles and laughter from a small group of kids under the watchful eyes of parents.

His nerves tempered, Chris mentally rehearses his speech until James declares, "It's time, and good luck!" He wades into the audience.

"Good lords and ladies," Chris says. "How many people know what a catapult is?" A sea of hands rises from the crowd. "All right. How many people know what a trebuchet is?" Not a single hand is raised.

"During medieval times wars were fought not so much by knight versus knight but as an army laying siege to a castle whose defensive designs had improved so much that a new offensive weapon was called for. Medieval engineers took a weapon that was originally designed by the Chinese and later improved by Arab engineers and enhanced it to become a fixed structure as large as a five-story building capable of hurling projectiles through castle walls, not over them.

"What does a trebuchet look like? Secured to and rising from a wheeled platform, trestles support an axle around which a massive beam pivots. One misconception is that the wheels transport the weapon great distances, which is not possible since the siege engine is too large to move from one kingdom to the next. Rather, they serve to increase the range of the projectile, to the surprise of many.

"How could a siege engine have such power? Like a seesaw, the trebuchet transfers energy from the descending end of the beam to the ascending end. Cut from a Douglas fir tree and octagonal in appearance, the beam, also known as a throwing arm, weighs close to two thousand pounds. When the weapon is primed, a thirteen-ton counterweight, which consists of a box-like container filled with sand, hangs near the rising end of the throwing arm, and attached to the opposite end of the beam is a long sling made of rope in which to hurl a large projectile.

"Unlike a seesaw, the beam's axle is suspended several stories high. Another difference is the side on which the counterweight attaches is a much shorter than that of the other.

"Once the trebuchet is unleashed, the great weapon groans as it rolls back and forth on its wheels as the counterweight, like a pendulum, sweeps well past its lowest point, greatly amplifying the arc of the opposite and longer end of the throwing arm to which a sling is attached. And the sling, which slides along a wooden channel that rests on the trebuchet's base before being whipped skyward, in turn amplifies the movement of the projectile. As a result, this double amplification enables a siege engine to hurl a 250-pound sandstone ball two hundred yards, pulverizing an enemy's castle wall.

"But it takes time to build the fearsome machine. Carpenters cut wood to make the base, capstans, trestles, and throwing arm.

Stonemasons quarry sandstone and carve projectiles, and timber framers secure major pieces to each other by connecting tonguelike appendages of one piece to a hole or slots of the other.

"As the parts are assembled over the course of several weeks, the trebuchet rises near the maximum range of rival archers and is shielded from their arrows. Facing a dilemma, enemy castle forces are compelled to launch a raid to destroy the siege engine or risk certain defeat after its completion.

"Today we are lucky to be able to reconstruct a trebuchet. Based on a few surviving thirteenth-century manuscripts and illustrations, several reproductions were built—some using modern materials and others using natural resources that were available during the same time period that validated its destructive power.

"For two hundred years the medieval siege engine reigned until cannons made it obsolete, and a new way to wage war began. Someday I hope to see a full-size replica at the fair and be in awe of it. Thank you."

Applause greets Chris, whose growing smile widens with each second of acclamation until he sees the jester knotted in discontent. His arms folded and his foot tapping, the fool immediately turns around and storms off in the opposite direction, his small hat bells ringing with every step.

A sense of betrayal rouses Chris's ire as he waves to the crowd for a few more moments and then hastily descends the wooden stairs and rejoins James at the landing.

"Why was the jester so unhappy again?" Chris demands.

"He usually speaks from up there," James says.

"What?" Chris exclaims. "I must have ruined his day! Why didn't you tell me?"

Taking a half step back, James hesitates and then responds calmly, "Trust me. You can never ruin the jester's day. He always has something bad to say about everyone, even if he or she has done everything right."

"Great, just what I need," Chris says, resigned to the idea. "Someone who can easily humiliate me in front of a large crowd."

"That is probably true," James says. "Regardless, if it weren't the jester, it would have been somebody else—colleagues, neighbors, or relatives. But that's part of the process of improving yourself. Not everyone will like you."

"Why?" Chris asks, his indignation ebbing.

"It could be hundreds of reasons," James muses. "Perhaps a few people in the audience wouldn't like to see others of similar talent get ahead of them. Or maybe people wouldn't like to hear what you had to say. But I am not going to spend all day speculating on which reason it would be. Instead of focusing on the one person who didn't like what you had to say, why not focus on the joy and sense of adventure that you brought to virtually the entire audience?"

Chris reflects on prudent advice, his outrage salved.

"Now, about your speech," James says, switching subjects, "you took a complicated topic—how a trebuchet works—and aptly described each component. You focused on one person at a time in the crowd, had a connection, and then moved on to someone else. I noticed that you used more gestures this time than last. Also, it was very impressive how you got the audience involved by asking a question at the very beginning and throughout your speech. This topic was really apropos to a medieval fair! As you could tell by the crowd's reaction, they really enjoyed your speech. Is there another one planned?"

"I hope not," Chris says, inwardly laughing at the thought. "I need to learn how to fight with a sword, not give speeches all day. I entered a tournament whose winner will be knighted late this afternoon."

"Fighting with a sword and shield?" James asks. "That's brave of you. What requires more bravery is speaking to the masses. That's why you should give another speech tomorrow. Obviously not here, but at another venue! Before I forget, good luck in the tournament."

"Thanks," Chris says, and the two shake hands and part ways.

As he retraces his steps across the courtyard, Chris looks at the placid sky and wonders whether it's an omen or an illusion, preceding storms to come. Soon he rejoins the wizard inside, who is still apparently reading the same oversized book lying on a lectern in front of the fireplace.

"How did it go?" the sage asks without looking up at his guest.

"The audience liked my speech," Chris says. "Didn't you hear the applause?"

"Yes," the wizard says. "Was that for you or someone else?"

"That was for me," Chris chafes.

"Good," the wizard says. "What was the subject of your speech?"

"I talked about how a trebuchet—" Chris explains.

Immediately the wizard's head snaps up. "A trebuchet?" he interjects. "What does a man who claims to have been in the heavens know about a trebuchet?"

"As an engineer," Chris says, his hand tracing the flight of an imaginary boulder, "I have been fascinated by projectiles."

With a sigh, the wizard looks down at his tome again and says, "Trebuchets are old news to me. Anyway, I am glad you gave two speeches. Let's see if you are willing to face your fears more often."

Pressed for time, Chris jokes, "If we don't meet your friend soon, perhaps you could wave your staff and make me a capable knight right now?"

"You, like royalty, want your fortunes changed in an instant!" the wizard admonishes in a commanding voice. "For you, learning one step at a time is best. No talismans of any kind, amulets, legendary swords, magic elixirs, or pixie dust will come to your aid. They cause too much trouble, and I spend a lifetime trying to undo the evil they create! I'm sorry. What is required of you involves a great deal of effort. In fact, people who fail have a shortcut mind-set."

Chris's grin evaporates.

Folding his arms in silhouette, the wizard says, "It was ages ago that out of the kindness of my heart, I helped someone much younger than you, though his situation was more compelling. He was a sailor blinded at the Battle of Sluys."

"I'm not familiar with that conflict," Chris says.

Shaking his head, the wizard says, "It doesn't matter. Warfare is all alike. Opposing forces engage, and the end result is the same. Countless people are killed, and scores injured, most of whom eventually die. In any event, when he was returned here, his livelihood was finished. Even worse, he had no family and turned to begging in the streets. I felt sorry for him and gave him a gift of wealth. But his dramatic change in fortune distorted his sense of self-worth. He led a lavish lifestyle, one that was unsustainable. There came a day when his debts exceeded his assets, and he ended up in the dungeon, where he perished. It's ironic that he was better off, despite his subsistence living, before I intervened and helped him. That's why I won't make the same mistake with you. They call this windfall *providence*."

"Windfalls happen," Chris says, who shrugs his shoulders and wonders about the sage's penchant for exaggeration. *If I've never heard of this battle before,* he thinks, *it must have occurred hundreds of years ago, or it's complete fiction. If this event did occur hundreds of years ago, does he honestly expect me to believe that he was alive then? Or is he just in character? I'll give him a pass for now.*

"Windfalls are shortcuts," the wizard says, "and these shortcuts leave you ill-prepared for future trials. You'll never know if you will measure up to the challenge." Leaning over toward Chris, the sage adds, "So as you see, gifts from heaven can actually stop or even delay one's development."

"Well—"

"All successful men have agreed in one thing—they were *causationists*. They believed that things went not by luck but by law; that there was not a weak or a cracked link in the chain that joins the first and last of things."[11]

"Good for them," Chris mutters, shifting his weight nervously. "Look, I was only kidding about enlisting your help to make me a suitable knight right away."

"Oh, you are not the only one who wants immediate change," the wizard says, still apparently not listening. "You should hear various members of royalty beseeching me. 'Can't you find a way to make me king?' 'Please grant me riches!' And my favorite, 'My forces are overwhelmed. Help me vanquish my enemy!' After I start granting people wishes, they want more. Riches acquired without effort will corrupt. Ever since I learned from my earlier attempt at generosity, I've found that it's a lot more challenging and rewarding when a person struggles to improve himself by dint of good, old-fashioned hard work. That individual seeks to improve his fate through the fruits of his labor rather than the magic of my staff. It's a refreshing change not having to cast a spell every day."

"It's not every day that you meet someone who's able to cast a spell," Chris says, not believing any of it.

Closing his book, apparently oblivious to the comment, the wizard says, "Now that you've overcome your fear of speaking to the populace, which happens to be man's greatest woe, one that people paradoxically fear more than death, you are truly brave! As a result, your remaining fears shouldn't take as much effort to overcome— which include battling demons—personal or otherwise. So now that you have passed the test, you can meet my friend. I think you'll be a changed man after you've finished your training. You will have many battles ahead—some against others, most against yourself. You will have fresh disciplines to learn, strangers to meet, and a new cause to follow—improving physically. If you feel your spirits flagging as you rise to meet your challenges or as you attempt to overcome your doubts and fears, I am here to help you. So consider me your friend."

"Thank you," Chris says graciously.

"By the way, did the king tell you what kind of weapon you will be using in the tournament?"

"No, but I assume it would be a sword," Chris says. "Will I be using a shield too?"

"That's just like the king," the wizard says with disdain. "He's all broad brushstrokes, and he leaves the details to those below him."

Chris shrugs.

"Your weapon is a *long* sword—one that requires two hands to wield," the wizard explains, "which means you will not be using a shield."

"Oh," Chris says. "Then how will I be able to defend myself?"

"Don't worry," the wizard says. "You'll be learning from an expert. Now follow me." He retrieves an apparent staff from the fireplace mantle and walks briskly out the door into the welcome sunshine.

At last, the tide has turned for Chris. It wouldn't be long until he would be preparing for the contest that held tantalizing possibilities. Perhaps he could break free of some childhood limitations with an instructor's help, for he expects a gauntlet of change awaits him.

Advancing across the courtyard with the help of his gnarled and weather-worn staff, which looks many times older than its bearer, the wizard heads toward the western wall. His pace quickening, Chris eventually catches up to the gray-bearded sage cloaked in a white robe and topped by a matching colored hat, brimmed and peaked. On his brow resides sagacity, and in his crescent eyes dwells discernment that's as keen as a hawk's.

The wizard, whose swiftness belies a frail frame and advanced age, complains, "Did you have a chance to see the castle yet? What were they thinking? It's not big enough! At best it would repel an army of dwarves."

"It's just for show," Chris ventures. "I don't think they were able to afford building a full-sized replica."

Glancing at Chris, the wizard says, "Not only does a man need a castle to protect himself against armies of his fellow men but also against the evil that lurks in the night—rogues, ruffians, brigands, miscreants, charlatans, knaves, and savage beasts. In fact, I fought a dragon less than a fortnight ago."

Stunned at the tall tale, Chris starts to gape and then says, "Right," his voice trailing off.

"It burned entire villages to the ground," the wizard says.

"Uh-huh," Chris mumbles halfheartedly.

"It will stop at nothing to—" the wizard says.

"You're laying it on too thick!" Chris interjects, fed up with this chimerical yarn. "I've put up with your nonsense long enough. If you want to be believed, stop telling these dragon tales!"

The two halt abruptly.

The wizard's visage flushes with anger. Many times he mouths words, but no sound comes from his lips. The sage takes a deep breath and then adds in a measured tone, "I will quit talking about dragons if you will stop babbling about your visit to the heavens."

"Done!" Chris exclaims, immediately accepting the offer. Thinking better of his remarks a few moments later, he adds, "Sorry I snapped. It's been a long day for me already, even at this early hour."

"Once a word has been allowed to escape, it cannot be recalled,"[12] the wizard says. "Let's hope that you don't treat my friend the same way. Otherwise I doubt that he would continue to instruct you," he says as the two resume their journey.

"Yes," Chris agrees, "but I'm sure I wouldn't do that."

Heading west along the courtyard, they approach a fortune-teller's booth on their right, which Chris points out and says, "Let's see what's going to happen to me today."

Instantly a look of dismay sweeps over the wizard's face. "You make your own future," he cautions. "It doesn't reveal itself by being predicted by someone who claims to know what will happen to you hours or days hence. Soothsayers!"

"Don't worry about me," Chris assures, indulging himself. "I'm a man of science. I need some entertainment right now."

"Go ahead," the wizard says with a scowl. "Enjoy yourself. But I can think of better forms of entertainment than this."

Confident that he will hear good news, Chris saunters over to the fortune-teller's booth that overflows with books and trinkets and orbs. Sitting at the counter is a man with snowy hair, knowing eyes, and a dimpled chin. He's garbed in a gray cloak and topped by a brimmed and pointed hat that is adorned by celestial bodies, near and far.

Upon his arrival, Chris asks the fortune-teller, "How much would it cost for me to find out whether I will win today's tournament to be a knight?"

A paroxysm of laughter overtakes the proprietor. Dejected, Chris slowly slinks away with his head down and trudges back to the wizard.

The sage hurries toward Chris, and when the two meet, the wizard says, "Maybe he just remembered a really funny joke."

"I doubt that," Chris growls, shaking his head in disbelief. "It's no fun being the laughingstock!"

"Heed not the scorn of others," the wizard says. "No one can make you feel inferior without your consent."[13]

Chris folds his arms, his face glum.

"I don't understand why you and your fellow visitors place such faith in the musings of a total stranger," the wizard says in bemusement. "Anyone here at the shire can assume that fellow's role."

"All right," Chris says, yielding to reason. Standing taller, he adds, "Since I have at least one upcoming battle later on today, I can't let what other people say get me down."

"Good," the wizard says. "Now follow me."

As they approach the courtyard's western edge, the wizard asks, "Do you see the gap in the wall that is protected by an iron gate over there?"

"Yes," Chris says.

"Beyond it lies a path that leads to my friend's training facility," the wizard says.

Intent on getting there as soon as possible, Chris exhorts, "Let's go!"

"Not so fast!" the wizard barks. He presses his staff against Chris to bar his way. "If you go down that path, there is one thing I can guarantee you, and that is failure, lots of it. What you spent your whole life avoiding awaits you beyond the gate. Are you sure that's what you want? To venture there?"

"I don't understand," Chris says. "All I'm going to do is learn how to wield a long sword. What's all this talk about failure?"

"Man errs as long as he strives,"[14] the wizard cautions. Looking at the portal, he adds, "So consider *erring* to be in abundance in your future, for it is a bitter fruit indeed. What might daunt you is that there will be much effort involved and that most of the time you are going to feel inferior by experiencing failure. Are you sure you want to go there?"

"Of course," Chris says. He will not be denied. He hikes over to the gate and tries to open it with one hand, but the portal doesn't budge. Then he uses both hands to no avail. For added leverage, he places his left foot on the stone wall and pulls with all his might, and slowly the gate opens. When the opening is wide enough, the wizard walks through followed closely by Chris.

CHAPTER 6

INTO THE LAND OF DESPAIR

The portal groans as it closes behind them.

As the two hike along a dirt path that extends beyond the southwest corner of the castle grounds, the noise of the crowd gradually recedes into the background. Soon they enter the woodlands where the protection of man from rival armies and savage beasts is no longer assured.

"I thought the landscape would look much different now that I've ventured into the forest where failure will dog me for the rest of the day," Chris gloats.

Looking around him, the wizard says, "I wouldn't be surprised if some incarnation of failure seeks you right now even as we speak."

Suddenly from behind a large boulder springs the very same jester Chris had seen minutes earlier in the courtyard. The fool's contrasting shoes, whose soles curl over his toes toward his ankles, do not help him stand taller. In fact, he is about four inches shorter than Chris.

Sauntering up to the novice, the jester rails with an English accent, "Did you realize that you gave a speech from *my* platform?

I can't believe you had the temerity to entertain the audience at my expense! What were you thinking?"

"Well, James told me I could," Chris says, pointing to the path that leads to the castle.

"James?" the jester says in astonishment. His eyes narrow as he looks upward as if searching for an answer. "I spent a few minutes in the privies and look what happened. He *encouraged* someone to entertain the crowd at my expense! So he still has a few more tricks up his sleeve after all. I'll deal with him later."

Confused, Chris says, "I saw you in the courtyard, but you didn't bother me about it until now. Why?"

"When people give their very first or second speech," the jester says, "their worst critic is their own inner voice. So you would not have heard anything I had to say. Now that you have some speeches under your belt and feel more confident about yourself, I am here to make sure that none remains as payback!"

A tremor of alarm courses through Chris.

"Don't you have better things to do like entertaining the king or his guests?" the wizard asks, stepping closer to the jester. "Why expend so much effort on an innocent mistake? James said that Chris could speak from your platform. How could Chris have known otherwise without James telling him?"

Adopting a softer tone, still tinged with contempt, the jester hisses, "Why should I let an upstart steal my thunder? Look what happened to James."

Curious, Chris asks, "What happened to him?"

"I replaced the old fool," the jester says, barely containing his delight.

"But this fellow is a visitor," the wizard says, extending an open hand toward Chris. "You needn't worry about him. He is in a contest whose champion will be knighted."

"Really?" the jester says. He begins to circle Chris, who suspects that the fool is sizing him up for another tongue-lashing. "What do you think you are doing here? Have you ever picked up a weapon in your life? Have you ever fought before?"

The wizard sighs and shakes his head.

"Yes, when I was a little kid," Chris says tentatively.

"Oh, when you were young, perhaps twenty or thirty years ago," the jester says, arching an eyebrow. "That's at least a generation ago!"

Like a contagion, the seed of doubt permeates Chris's mind, sapping his tenacity, undermining his resolve.

"But you are an adult now," the jester says. "Speaking of adults, do you think that you will be better than the other contenders?"

"Of course," Chris says guardedly.

"Give me some reasons," the jester suggests, his lips curving into an upturned smile.

"Well—" Chris says, stalling for time. Finally he adds, "I'm optimistic."

"This is combat," the jester says. "You do not have the build of a fighter. I'd imagine that the other challengers are a lot younger and stronger than you." Drawing nearer, he approaches Chris to within an arm's length. "Let me take a closer look at you. Average height, average weight, and a below-average build. There's nothing remarkable about you! An average person you will be. But becoming a knight requires superior strength and stamina, none of which you appear to have."

Chris draws his hand to his chin, mulls it over momentarily, and then ventures softly, "Maybe I made a mistake. Perhaps I shouldn't be here. I should have stayed with the rest of the visitors and enjoyed myself."

The jester flashes a devilish grin.

The wizard leans slowly toward Chris and whispers, "Where's your courage? You gave up so easily, and you haven't even lifted a weapon yet."

"The jester is right," Chris says with a sigh. "I don't think I can do it."

His head drooping and then motioning toward the path, the wizard exhorts, "Come with me. I'll change your mind."

The jester, whose lips quickly curl into a frown, admonishes, "You haven't seen the last of me!" His eyes downcast, he wanders away.

For a short while Chris and the sage head west, trudging up an incline. They eventually reach the crest of a distant hill shaded by a stand of oak trees.

Rubbing his eyes with his left hand, the wizard says, "That fool didn't disclose any new information that you didn't already know."

"The jester made such a big deal out of my lack of measuring up in every way," Chris says, looking at the old man with weariness. "I figured he's an expert. I am sure he has seen competitors come and go."

"Who cares what he thinks," the wizard scoffs. "Public opinion is a weak tyrant compared with our own private opinion. What a man thinks of himself, that it is which determines, or rather, indicates, his fate."[15]

"All right, I won't care about *his* opinion about my abilities," Chris says. "But what's his beef with me?"

Lifting his index finger, the wizard says calmly, "He's a one-man show in the courtyard. So don't be surprised if he gets angry at you for invading his turf."

"How does he expect anyone to improve if he is constantly tearing them down?" Chris asks, incredulous.

"That's the point," the wizard says, motioning his staff emphatically. "He doesn't want anyone else to compete with him. If you are going to learn how to speak to the crowd on *his* turf, expect a scrap."

"Yes," Chris agrees, his arms outstretched, "and he'll be able to make fun of me in front of hundreds of people."

"That's what he does for a living," the wizard mutters. "That's life."

"Life's unfair," Chris says with a look of disillusionment.

"Here is your first obstacle of today," the wizard says, pointing at Chris. "Do not let it defeat you. Why do you cling to the idea that everyone will face the same opportunities and challenges? The situation simply doesn't exist. Even for newborns, life isn't fair. Few babies are born to royal families. Most aren't."

Baffled, Chris says, "But I am not battling royalty today."

"Indeed," the wizard says. "Those young commoners find their specialty elsewhere. Some are artistic, athletic, gregarious, and pugnacious, just to name a few. Life has a way of educating them really fast. But the smartest ones take steps to advance their lot in life to further their trade or to increase their knowledge of other pursuits."

His eyes expanding, Chris asks, "How do they accomplish that?"

"They read books," the wizard says. "How many have you read to improve your physique or your endurance?"

"Just one."

"Woe be to him that reads but one book,"[16] the wizard cautions. "You should read more!"

"But I've read plenty of engineering books," Chris explains, "which helped me gain the necessary knowledge to build my experiment. But your advice is for those who have a lot of time on their hands, and I'm too busy to read them."

"You wish to advance through life without their counsel?" the wizard asks.

"All right. I'll make time to read them on the weekends, but I won't have as much time to relax."

"Weekends? What are they?"

"Oh, never mind."

"But I still don't understand why you don't have the time to do such things," the wizard says with a quizzical look. "Do you think your kingdom will flourish while you relax?"

"Probably not," Chris says without much thought.

"Then behold your sovereign's kingdom," the wizard declares, "which extends beyond the horizon in all directions."

Playing along, Chris looks at the wide sweep of country from the distant castle to the crystalline lake and adjacent mountains, for the alpine air is intoxicating, the Arcadian landscape relaxing.

"Every man is the architect of his own fortune,"[17] the wizard says, extending an open hand toward the horizon. "How robust *your* kingdom will be depends on how hard you work now. And you said your kingdom was lacking."

Chris looks at nature's grandeur for a few seconds and then turns to the wizard and admits, "Yes, I said that. But I really have my doubts about being the architect of my fortune."

"Why is that?" the wizard asks.

Chris hesitates and then says, "I know we agreed not to discuss certain subjects, but others will determine whether I'll get another opportunity to venture into space again."

The wizard hems for a moment, collects himself, and then says, "All right. I'll entertain the notion just this time. So what if you don't? Move on and find something else to do."

"Since I've been in space, there's no way I'm going to top that," Chris says, looking at the sky. "Anything else would seem like child's play."

"That may be so," the wizard says. "Ultimately, you must decide what you will do next with your life."

"Well, I don't know what to do next," Chris says as a sense of gloom overtakes him.

"Let each man exercise the art he knows,"[18] the wizard says.

"My art is science," Chris explains. "Any other field I don't know that much about."

"If you've ruled out your calling, then consider working for others who know their craft well," the wizard suggests. "Make yourself necessary to somebody."[19]

"I've worked for others long enough," Chris says, sapped of energy. "That no longer interests me."

"That doesn't leave much else," the wizard says. He slowly walks away while he mutters to himself. Abruptly the sage's head rears back, as if jolted by electricity. He turns around, his eyes brightening. "Since you have just excluded opportunities that you have observed during your adult life, perhaps then you should harken back to your childhood. Take a look around you. Perhaps it has been ages since you have wandered out into the woods in wonder. Her trees loom large and need to be scaled, her thoroughfares traversed, her crags clambered, her streams and ponds explored for aquatic life, and her resources fashioned into a fortress that offers protection from the evil that lurks in the night." Pointing at Chris's torso, the wizard adds, "The great man is he who does not lose his child's heart."[20]

Perplexed, Chris says, "I don't see the connection between childhood and adulthood, where one pursues a profession."

"As a child, you could imagine many things that were possible, and no one else could tell you otherwise. Presumably whatever you envisioned is something that you would like to do."

"I've become jaded after forty-one years."

"You asked me to indulge in your notion of your trip into the heavens," the wizard says, glancing skyward. "Now it's your turn to prepare for the possibility that it may not happen again. Perhaps the universe no longer holds your attention. Consider an inward journey or some sort of personal attainment."

Chris thinks about the subject at length. Finally he admits, "Because a lot of kids bullied me when I was little and because I haven't done anything to improve my strength for my own misguided reasons, I would like to master the martial arts."

"How do you know about that discipline?" the wizard inquires as wrinkles crease his brow. "It's practiced thousands of miles to the east. No one performs it in these parts."

Not wishing to start an argument, Chris dismisses the concern, saying, "Don't worry. I'll find one, but that is for another day. As for today, I have a lot to do."

"Good luck finding one," the wizard says sarcastically.

Chris nods.

Farther up the trail, the sound of whinnying horses abounds. Soon two princes appear, resplendent in scarlet-and-gold finery, riding on horseback toward them.

As the two on foot get out of the way, the wizard says, "Another way to get around a want of a noble lineage or royal education is seeking expert advice. Oh, and I nearly forgot to mention this," the sage cautions. "Never trust the advice of a man in difficulties."[21]

"What do you mean?" Chris asks, his eyes squinting from incomprehension.

"For example," the wizard says, "never take business advice from somebody whose business is failing or someone in a dungeon because of a business failure."

"Oh, I get the idea," Chris says, playing along.

"So you see, by reading books and consulting with experts, you can apply that knowledge and overcome your humble beginnings as a commoner. As a result, you can't say that life isn't fair because the remedies to life's inequities are readily within your grasp."

"I think you're making it sound easier than it actually is," Chris says, not quite a believer.

"You have it easier than most," the wizard says. Pointing to Chris's head, the sage adds, "Judging by the health of your teeth, you are not an indentured servant. No doubt that wherever you hail from, books are as plentiful as the stars in the sky."

Not one to concede the point so easily since his childhood incidents have been his crutch for many decades, Chris ponders the issue further.

"There are two guarantees in life," the wizard says, "and life being fair isn't one of them. The sooner you accept that, the quicker you will get on with your life and *do* what is best for you instead of *complaining* about it."

"Since I won't have time to read a book today, I'll have to rely on an expert."

"And so you shall," the wizard says. "His name is Pierce. Now let's go see him."

Heading deeper into the forest, they follow a descending path, and around them nature's sounds become more pronounced—the piping of various birds, the pitter-patter of falling leaves, the creaking of trees during sporadic wind gusts, the occasional clatter of fleeing squirrels, and the frequent snap of twigs underfoot. Surprised by the solitude, Chris asks, "How come there's hardly anyone around here?"

Shrugging slightly, the wizard says, "It's outside the fairgrounds. The few people who venture here discover that fighting with a long sword requires an entire day's commitment. Then they promptly turn around and head back to the festival to enjoy themselves."

For a short while longer, they enjoy dappled sunlight until they approach the forest's edge where the intermittent sound of clashing swords along with curt instructions greets Chris's ears. And a foreboding seven-foot giant with tousled russet hair and a shaggy beard greets Chris's eyes.

"The jester sends his regards," the giant rumbles ominously in an English tone. Draped in a gray tunic that's tattered from overuse, he approaches them.

The wizard's look of concern becomes one of apprehension as the looming figure draws closer. Lifting his staff, the sage cautions, "You'd better think again of whatever mischief that you have planned."

Without breaking his stride, the giant says, "Legend has it that you haven't used that prop in your hand for ages." As the giant almost reaches them, he adds, "Why should I be afraid?"

A frisson surges through Chris like electricity. But he's not sure whom the giant is pursuing. Or is he playing a prank on them? At the last moment the giant lunges at Chris, snatches him by the ankle with an immense hand, and hoists him unceremoniously into the air.

Pointing to Chris with his free hand while leaning over the wizard, the giant, whose face grows menacing, says, "The jester thought I would be more persuasive than he was. Chris needs to leave the kingdom now, or you'll be dealing with me again. The next time I see him, I won't be so nice!"

Looking up at the titan, the wizard says, "No giant would ever submit to the jester's bidding. How has he turned you?"

"Let me go!" Chris interjects, contorting his torso in an effort to free himself from the giant's clutches. But Chris is too weak to do so.

"He's blackmailing me," the giant says to the wizard.

"How?" the wizard asks.

Chris makes a few more feeble attempts to free his ankle from the giant's grasp but dangles back to earth each time. Frustrated, Chris yells louder, "Let me go!"

"He knows where I live," the giant says to the wizard, "and we both have a criminal past. We plundered travelers in the forest until he figured out that he would have a better life in a castle making fun of people than dwelling in the forest, always on the run. Everyone would believe my guilt, but hardly a soul would believe his."

"The king will believe me, as I am his counselor," the wizard explains, who groans as he reaches up to pat the giant on his upper right arm. "So you will not have to worry about your past anymore unless you are still a brigand."

"No," the giant says crisply.

"Good. What do you do now?"

"I work in the quarries."

"Why not go to another kingdom?"

"They might consider me an assassin or a spy, both of which have bad endings."

Hopeful that his calm entreaty will be heeded, Chris interrupts, pleading, "I really need to get down now because my foot is starting to feel numb."

The leviathan hesitates.

"The king would not look kindly upon you if you disabled one of his challengers before the tournament starts," the wizard says, pointing his staff at Chris. "Indeed, the king might view an assault on one of the competitors that he personally selected as an attack upon his kingdom. I suppose that the monarch would muster all the resources at his disposal to hunt you down and kill you forthwith!"

"All right," the giant says and lowers Chris to the ground.

Angrily dusting himself off, Chris demands, "What other friends does the jester have that I should be concerned with?"

"He has a few more," the giant says, his faint smile growing wider, "but none with my size or strength."

"Good," the wizard says. He turns to Chris and says, "You don't have to worry about hanging upside down again." Addressing the giant, the sage adds, "Now that you no longer need to fear the jester, why don't you join us as I introduce Chris to his new instructor?"

"To help Chris win the tournament?" the giant asks.

The wizard nods.

"All right," the giant says. "Let's go."

* * *

A carpet of fragrant grass unfurls across a bluff, its margins lined with tidy hedges that overlook the lake—a taunting tableau of relaxation agonizingly nearby. A refreshing zephyr sweeps across the lawn, rustling the leaves on the neighboring trees from which birds warble, and the late-morning sun marches inexorably across the clear blue sky.

Chris spots an instructor he assumes to be Pierce, who is training a group of students. During the lesson Chris wanders near the edge of the precipice to enjoy the view. But the frenetic masses below him capture his attention. The king's army hones its skills on a wide field extending to the lake.

In front of him near the lakeshore, longbow men—perhaps at least a hundred strong gathered into nine groups—practice their craft against a multitude of distant targets. To his right, a dozen mounted knights take their turn trying to strike a small stationary target with their lances. Directly below him, scores of mounted knights race along an open field, sending a trail of dust high into the sky. Off to his left, opposing troops on foot attack each another in a mock battle, and diagonally to his left near the forest's edge and adjacent to the lakeshore, fully armored knights are paired off in formalized one-on-one training. *Perhaps at least one of my fellow contestants is out there*, Chris wonders.

"Would you like to join them?" the wizard asks, drawing up next to the apprentice.

"No," Chris says without much thought. "I'm not a knight yet."

Motioning toward the woods, the wizard asks, "Back there, I trust there are no ill effects from hanging upside down for a while?"

"It was really depressing that he could lift me with one hand. I wasn't strong enough to bend up from my waist and find some way to free my foot or inflict some pain on his torso."

"I suppose all of us feel the same way. But I can't imagine anyone being taller, and if he's been quarrying rock for some time, perhaps no one is stronger. But height and strength can be overcome. If we travel farther to the east, another friend of mine could tell you how to break his knees, and then the giant would seem neither as tall nor as strong. But that is for another day."

Turning to the giant, the wizard says, "Don't worry. We're not plotting against you."

"You wouldn't be the first," the giant says, lifting his chin subtly.

Chris says to the wizard, "But you should also know that I have a problem fighting others as well. You see, when I was as a little kid, I got bullied a lot. In fact, one time I got into a fight and was knocked out. Ever since then, I have been a wimp. Physically I never amounted to much."

"Oh, you give that event too much credence," the wizard says in a paternal tone. "Waste not fresh tears over old griefs."[22]

"No, you don't understand," Chris says, growing irritated. "It *did* have a big impact on my life. That's why I've channeled my energy into science. I have never been good in a physical tournament, only research. That's why it was so easy for the jester to convince me that I had no chance in this tournament."

"Everyone experiences a setback of some kind, an illness or injury, a diminished quality of life, a handicap, or a loss of some kind—mental or otherwise," the wizard says. Then he adds, "An injury is much sooner forgotten than an insult."[23]

"I was knocked out," Chris says with growing resentment. "The only defeat worse than that is getting killed!"

"Since you are among the living," the wizard says, "while there's life, there's hope."[24] His eyes narrowing, he adds, "What else did you learn from that experience other than that you could never be very good at anything physically?"

After much consideration, Chris says, "Nothing."

"Look at the sky," the wizard beckons. "Don't you find it odd that celestial objects—the sun, moon, and stars—draw your interest while your body remains neglected? I imagine that you would be a more robust man today if you had simply moved on." Looking heavenward, the wizard declares, "He knows the universe, and himself he does not know."[25] Shifting his attention back to Chris again, the wizard asks, "Haven't you done anything recently to make your body stronger?" Motioning to the forest around them, he asks, "Have you ever felled trees, hewn wood, chiseled rock?"

"No, I haven't because I feel more comfortable studying science."

"Everyone has an excuse," the wizard says. "We know the good, we apprehend it clearly, but we can't bring it to achievement."[26]

"I had my reasons."

"You battled a youngster and lost *ages* ago!"

"He was taller than I was!"

"That youth did more damage to your soul than this giant ever could," the wizard says.

Chris draws a sharp breath. *Possibly the wizard is right*, he reckons. Adding his justification for not changing his ways, Chris says, "Well, we all learn from the past."

"Experience keeps a dear school, yet fools will learn in no other,"[27] the wizard says.

"Experience taught me a bitter lesson!" Chris snarls.

"Indeed—for a day, a week, maybe a fortnight," the wizard says, patting Chris on his back. "Obviously you've healed from your injuries while your bitter defeat has endured for decades." Adopting a softer tone, the sage adds, "The greatest griefs are those we cause ourselves."[28]

Chris looks at the ground in disgust. Swallowing his pride, he asks, "Okay, so what should I change?"

"For starters," the wizard says, "you incorrectly compared yourself to others—someone of Herculean strength. Also, you knew what to do as far as making your body stronger, but you didn't act upon it. Finally you've allowed this experience to define you and dictate your future. The confluence of missteps has conspired against you." Motioning to the lake, he adds, "Ill habits gather by unseen degrees—as brooks make rivers, rivers run to seas."[29]

"Is it any wonder then that I haven't changed?" Chris asks. "With your guidance, I can get rid of them all at once."

"I think you've overestimated my powers," the wizard says, lifting his staff.

"How's that?" Chris asks.

"Habit is habit, and not to be flung out of the window by any man, but coaxed downstairs a step at a time,"[30] the wizard says. "You would be attempting to do too much at the same time! If you've ever tried juggling, I'm sure that would be apparent to you. In fact, that sounds like a good idea. Fortunately there is a juggler in these parts. You should see her sometime today. In any event, the day grows late. Change awaits you, my friend."

CHAPTER 7

THE LONG SWORD AND THE APPRENTICE

With an emphatic swing of his weapon, his armor glinting in the sunlight, the instructor appears to have finished his lesson. From behind the expert, the wizard calls out to him, "Pierce! There are two people I would like you to meet."

Facing a class of thirty students, the instructor exclaims in an English dialect, "I recognize that voice! Everyone, take fifteen minutes to practice these moves against one another, and I'll see you next year. Many thanks for your patronage. Carry on." Pierce, who cuts an imposing figure, turns around and approaches the trio. No doubt he is blessed—graced with a sonorous voice, a barrel-sized chest, and an assured demeanor. "Glad to see you!" he says effusively. "Who are your friends?"

Extending an open palm toward the novice, the wizard says, "Pierce, I'd like to introduce you to Chris, and ... uh, this giant."

Turning to Chris, the wizard says, "This is my friend Pierce, who's an expert at wielding a long sword."

"Hi," Pierce says. He shakes Chris's hand firmly and then hesitates before he finally shakes the giant's. The instructor adds,

"I don't think this tall fellow will be able to find a suit of armor big enough to fit him."

"No need to worry about that," the wizard says. "He's not in the tournament. Anyway, my friend Chris needs help. The king chose him as a contender in a tournament whose victor will be knighted late this afternoon. Would you have the time to train him?"

"Does he have any experience?" Pierce asks.

"No," the wizard says in a low voice. "He'll be starting from scratch."

In an upbeat tone, Pierce says, "All my students who eventually became experts had to start as novices. Yes, I can train him. But I'll have to find another day to go fishing." Pierce looks at Chris and asks, "So you want to join the realm?"

"Yes, I do!" Chris says with a nod. "Thank you for those encouraging words. I am sure there is a lot for me to learn. It's time for me to change," he says, glancing at the wizard.

"And so you shall," Pierce says. "Now let's get started."

"Before you go," the wizard interjects, "perhaps this giant could be of some assistance to you. I'm sure you could find him something less strenuous to do than splitting stones."

"Yes," Pierce says. "Since this is the last day of the fair, I'll need some help removing and storing equipment."

Nodding subtly, the wizard says, "Chris, you are in good hands. My help is no longer needed. Good luck!"

Chris waves his hand and says, "Thanks for your help!"

"Good seeing you again, Pierce," the wizard says, hefting his staff.

Raising his weapon, Pierce says, "Great to see you."

Slowly the wizard turns around and heads back to the fair.

Looking at the giant, Pierce says, "Why don't you hang around and watch me instruct Chris for a while until there is a break in his training. Then I'll have a chance to show you where to store all the equipment until next season."

"All right," the giant says.

Addressing Chris, Pierce says, "Let's get started." He sheathes what the apprentice assumes to be a long sword. "A few things about your weapon—it will help you on your quest to become a knight."

"Obviously," Chris says, his forehead riddled with creases.

"Your implement doesn't care whether you practice, whether you learn from your mistakes, or how well you use your time. It doesn't care if you have had a rotten childhood, failed at your business, fell ill during adulthood, or seen death up close upon a battlefield. So, how well you use your weapon today will determine how far you advance."

Chris nods.

"To succeed at swordsmanship, you need strength and stamina. You'll need stamina to swing away at your opponent for minutes on end. Since you have not yet learned a single strike, to increase your endurance, why don't you run flat out like Usain Bolt around the field here instead?"

Stung by the remark, Chris glares at his instructor and says, "Look, don't start with what it looks like at the top of the mountain— like so-and-so won X gold medals or has ten homes, three businesses, and retired at fifty. Instead commence at foothills looking up at the mountain. Start with me, not them! Begin with my abilities. Give me a plan for change and a timetable for that to happen."

"So you want to learn how to summit your own Mount Everest?" Pierce asks.

"Yes!" Chris says. "That is a good way of putting it."

"All right," Pierce says. "We'll discuss your timetable later." Pointing out the boundaries, he adds, "Since it's only about a hundred yards around the perimeter of the field, I think you could run several laps. Would you like to have a go at it?"

"Sure."

"How many laps do you think you can do?"

"About five," Chris ventures.

"Are you sure?" Pierce asks.

"Now that you mention it," an emboldened Chris reckons, "I think I am capable of seven."

"Good luck to you!" Pierce says. Motioning toward the clearing, he adds, "Let's see how many you can really do."

"Thanks," Chris says as he starts to jog away.

On his first lap he runs briskly. His pace slowing, the apprentice completes his second lap. As he makes his third trip around the perimeter of the field, his breathing becomes labored.

"You need to be *focused*," Pierce says without much conviction. "Do you want it badly enough?" He falls silent for a few moments and then adds, "Pick up the pace. You could be chasing after your next meal!"

Eventually Chris succumbs to exhaustion and stops on his fourth lap, doubled over while trying to catch his breath just a few yards away from his instructor.

"That didn't work," Pierce says in mock surprise. "You're knackered. So you need to improve your stamina."

"Knackered, huh?" Chris says, panting and trying to keep down his last meal. "But I've got all day."

"Since there is only so much that you can do during the limited time leading up to the tournament," Pierce explains, "your stamina will only improve a little. I don't want to give you a heart attack. You have not even engaged in combat yet. So I'll let you catch your breath."

Chris's breathing returns to normal after a few minutes, and then he asks, "Okay, what's next?"

Pointing to a nearby table upon which many weapons and training instruments are displayed, Pierce says, "Let's have a look at what you'll be using today."

"All right," Chris says, and the two head in that direction.

With the giant trailing far behind, the master and apprentice draw up to the table. "When I was in your shoes first starting out," Pierce says, "it seemed so overwhelming."

Chris nods.

"Depending on whether you are practicing your stances alone, sparing against others, or participating in a tournament will dictate which implement you will be using, none of which requires wielding an actual long sword. So let me show you a real one first."

Pierce retrieves the closest weapon, a forty-inch-long, parallel-edged long sword by its seven-inch handle from the table, its blade gleaming in the sunlight. "Here's one," he says. "But first I want to demonstrate how pliable the blade is." He returns the weapon to the table with the blade at its midpoint extending over the edge. Pierce grasps the handle with one hand, bends the tip of the long sword a few inches toward the ground with the other, and lets it go.

Chris watches the weapon oscillate toward its true line.

"You see," Pierce says, "the blade is more flexible than you thought it was. Another misconception is that most people assume that a long sword weighs ten to twenty pounds. Actually the weight is closer to two-and-a-half to three-and-a-half pounds. So you needn't be a hulk or a barbarian to wield it."

"That's good news since no one will mistake me for either of those two," Chris says with a twisted smile.

Pierce hands the weapon to Chris and says, "I want you to know what a real long sword feels like before you wield the first of several training implements. Feel how well balanced it is."

Chris grasps the weapon with both hands and says, "I'm glad I don't have to be incredibly strong to wield this."

"Not only strength, but also stamina and quickness," Pierce corrects. "Cunning helps too. When I give you your blunt a few moments from now, you will notice that it weighs more."

Chris takes a few swipes at an imaginary target.

"Now that you appreciate the finer qualities of a real long sword," Pierce says, "let me show you the other implements that you'll be using today." Chris hands the long sword to Pierce, who returns it to the table.

Lifting the next weapon, Pierce explains, "For the tournament you will be using a padded long sword—one cushioned by closed-cell, high-impact foam. Don't worry. You'll have plenty of time to use this weapon later on today." He lays the canvas-covered implement back onto the table and then retrieves another weapon and hands it to Chris.

"This is a blunt," Pierce says, "an extra-thick, inflexible, and heavier-than-normal long sword with smooth edges so that you won't be able to cut your opponent and a rounded edge at the tip so that you will not be able to stab anyone with it."

Nodding, Chris says, "Right." Wielding the weapon, he slashes an invisible foe.

"By the way," Pierce says, "you won't be engaging in full-contact sparing using a blunt or a real long sword during today's tournament."

"Why not?" Chris asks.

"It's too dangerous!" Pierce cautions.

"All right," Chris says sheepishly, "I'll take your word for it."

"Anyway," Pierce says, "the blunt is useful to teach you stances and allows you to feel steel-on-steel contact that you wouldn't be able to simulate if you were practicing with wood."

"Wood?" Chris echoes incredulously.

"Yes," Pierce says. He exchanges the blunt from Chris for a wooden weapon and lays the blunt on the table. "A student should use a wooden weapon for practice—without an adversary in front of him. It is closer to the actual weight and feel of a real long sword but obviously has no sharp edges."

"I see," Chris says.

"Now that I've shown you what you'll be training with," Pierce says, "it's time for me to teach you the various stances that you'll need to master before today's match."

Chris nods.

"Since you won't be using a real long sword," Pierce says, "which is fairly light, you won't need to train as much with this similarly weighted wooden weapon. Instead, you'll start with your blunt to learn these stances." He exchanges weapons with Chris and returns the wooden implement to the table.

* * *

Slowly the shadows retreat as the sun climbs higher in the sky, and the trees continue to heap their autumnal bounty upon the cluttered ground.

Through difficulty, the student steadily progresses until he is ready for a review of the primary stances. Pierce says, "Let's see how much you remember. Right-back guard, middle guard, high guard, left-hanging guard." Chris correctly assumes each stance.

"Great!" Pierce says. "Are you ready for a break?"

"Of course," Chris says.

"Good," Pierce says. "Take forty-five minutes. Let's see if you remember what I taught you when you return."

Mentally fatigued, Chris says, "Thanks," and returns his blunt to the table.

"By the way," Pierce says, "if you want a change of pace, go to the indoor archery range just beyond the courtyard."

Glad to mix some enjoyment during his training, Chris says, "Sounds like a good idea," and returns to the path leading back to the fair.

Crossing the field and into the shade of the still forest for most of the journey, Chris makes his way back to the courtyard gate, which oddly doesn't offer much resistance when he opens it. Now the quad seems much larger, for the morning crowds have dwindled. To his delight, his adversary is nowhere to be seen.

Exiting the courtyard, Chris follows the signs to an indoor archery range, where he ambles over to an instructor who casts a gimlet eye on her students. Seeking an audience, Chris says, "Excuse me. I would like to try my luck at archery today."

A titian-haired woman adorned in a brown sleeveless surcoat worn over a chalky tunic meets Chris's gaze. She says in an English, velvety voice, "Hi, I am Sarah. You're not from these parts, are you?"

"No, I'm far from home."

"I figured as much. In any event, you'll need to try your luck at striking the dragon's heart—the little white area on his red body. To do so, you'll need the tools of the trade. Now if you'll follow me."

Taking a look at a target, Chris judges the dragon's heart to be roughly a third of the size of a bull's-eye. "That's what I need," he says, trailing slightly behind her, "a stationary foe that doesn't fight back."

She chuckles and then asks, "So what brings you here today?"

"Do you know Pierce?"

"Yes, he stops by now and then."

"He's teaching me how to wield a long sword," Chris says, "and I'm on my break."

Nodding subtlety, Sarah asks, "Did you know that arrows can pierce armor? Why would you engage in such an endeavor when armor offers no protection from arrows? Have you learned nothing from the Battle of Crécy?"

"Yes, the king mentioned it this morning," Chris recalls. "But he chose me as a contestant to be a knight, not a longbowman. So I'll have to make do."

"I suppose the king wants to keep all the elements of his army," she says softly.

"What got you interested in archery?" Chris asks.

"My father was at the Battle of Crécy and the Battle of Poitiers," she says, her voice infused with pride. Upon reaching the equipment storage room, she turns to Chris and adds, "But I needed to protect myself and my family somehow while he was away. So this is what I mastered."

"I suppose we must become an expert at a new skill because something unexpected happened to us," Chris says, going with the flow.

Sarah takes a deep breath. "Anyway, back to the present," she says. Pointing to the archery gear, she adds, "Grab this bow. I'll secure your quiver and tie a guard on your left forearm."

During the fitting, the twang of bowstrings and thudding of arrows into their targets fill the air.

As the two stroll over to a vacant stand, Chris wonders whether his aim is good enough to actually hit the dragon with one of his arrows.

"You can stand right here," Sarah beckons. "Make sure you stand perpendicular to the target."

Getting ready to fire, Chris switches the bow to his left hand and draws an arrow from his quiver with his right.

"Just try your best to strike the dragon's heart," Sarah suggests.

"All right," Chris says. He places an arrow on the bowstring, draws it back, and fires, missing the dragon to the left.

"Don't worry," Sarah says. "That was your first shot. Forget about that one and try again."

Chris shrugs his shoulders. He looses another arrow, which lands well below the target.

"Missed again," Chris growls.

"So what?" Sarah says. "The last two arrows won't predict where the next one will end up."

"All right," Chris grumbles. Again he fires another arrow, sending it a foot above the demon.

Frustrated, Chris asks, "What if I move closer to the target to build up my confidence?"

"You could be shot in the back by your fellow archers," Sarah cautions. "Anyway, don't worry. You've only shot three arrows. Figure out where your aim is and where the arrow lands and make an adjustment."

Chris nods. He looses another arrow, which lands wide left of the target again. Shaking his head, he attempts to give Sarah his bow and says, "That target is too small for me to hit. I can't do this."

Folding her arms, Sarah says, "When the archer misses the center of the target, he turns round and seeks for the cause of his failure in himself."[31]

Chris lets out a long sigh and then lowers his bow to his side. "All right. What do I need to do that I haven't tried already?"

"For starters," Sarah says, "make sure to lock your left elbow before you release the bowstring, and try holding your breath."

Mustering new resolve, Chris says, "Okay, I'll try that." Slowly he turns around to face his target. He readies another arrow, holds his breath for a moment, locks his left elbow, and releases the missile, which hits the dragon's tail.

Pleasantly surprised, Chris observes, "At least I hit the target."

Nodding, Sarah says, "Yes, that's encouraging, and with practice, you'll slay the demon by piercing its heart."

"I think I should quit while I'm ahead," Chris says, nodding.

"If that's what you want," Sarah says with an undertone of displeasure in her voice.

"Yes, it is," Chris says. He leads the way back to the equipment locker, where he returns his gear.

"Sorry, but my time is up," Chris says, guessing that his break will be over by the time he sees Pierce again. "Since this is the last day of the fair, I will have to pick up the sport another time. Thanks for the lesson," and then he shakes her hand.

"You are welcome and good luck in the tournament!" Sarah says.

"Thanks!" Chris says. He turns around and makes his way back to the courtyard gate and then follows the path into the forest.

Walking through the sylvan realm, painted in pine green and fiery hues, he enjoys the brief respite before the day's rigors resume. Soon he rejoins his instructor waiting for him on the bluff.

"Glad to see you're back," Pierce says, grinning. "How was it? Did you have fun?"

"I had to eat humble pie," Chris says. "I had a shaky start, but I eventually hit the target."

"Good," Pierce says, returning the blunt to his student. "Perhaps someday you'll be able to hit a *moving* target with an arrow and be one up on her. I would imagine that you could use that skill to hunt small game with a crossbow and be self-sufficient."

Chris chuckles and then says, "I really don't plan on living in the woods just yet."

"Your life depends on others being able to perform their duties," Pierce cautions. "If they cannot, you won't survive long."

Wanting to sidestep the issue and guessing that the details of his last encounter would get Pierce's goat, Chris says, "By the way, during my break my instructor told me that the arrow was superior to armor."

"What rubbish!" Pierce exclaims with a scowl. "Now I understand that her conversations with me were merely professional courtesy. She revealed her true feelings to you." Mimicking the posture of an archer, he growls, "Longbows derive their advantage sheerly by launching their weapons in mass volleys. The craft doesn't require one to even aim at individual targets. Archers just hope their enemy is still gathered where their arrows fall. Do you see any practical application for shooting at *stationary* targets? I don't. The only war I know is one that is fluid, ever-changing."

Suspecting that Pierce has firsthand experience, Chris says, "I'm glad to know that I was chosen for a superior form of combat," guessing otherwise.

With a sigh, Pierce says, "It appears that her remark got the better of me. I'm sorry, Chris. Are you ready to learn the transitional stances—those that take you from one primary position to the next—and the different angles of striking an opponent that each stance affords?"

"Sure," Chris says, glad to be on track with his training.

Again the instructor demonstrates, and the student follows, which continues for an hour. To complete his student's training, Pierce teaches parries and in slow arcs swings his blunt at Chris in simulated attacks.

"You are doing well," Pierce says. "Looks like you need another break." Chris relaxes his body and lowers his guard. Retiring his weapon to a nearby table, Pierce inquires, "So when you are not on holiday, what do you do?"

"Unfortunately," Chris says, "before I had a chance to complete my mission at the space station and deploy my two small satellites that I designed, I banged my head against a hatch during an emergency. The crew brought me back to Earth as soon as they could. So here I am."

"Sorry to hear about what happened to you, but it seems to me as if you're okay. Is that correct?"

"Yes."

"I didn't know that you're an astronaut. Wow, that's exciting. You must have trained a long time for your mission."

"Not really. About three months."

His eyes wide, Pierce says, "I thought astronauts trained for years."

"You must have me confused with career astronauts," Chris says. "I'm a noncareer astronaut. I was responsible for deploying my payload and making sure that it worked before the end of the mission. Unfortunately that didn't happen."

"Right," Pierce says. "Regardless of the outcome, what you engineered sounds impressive. How do you go from designing small satellites to fighting with long swords?"

"Physical fitness was never my strong point ever since I got knocked out as a kid," Chris says.

"We all take our lumps," Pierce says. "Besides, you're a lot older now, and you will be wielding a padded long sword. Perhaps your fortune will change today."

"I hope so too," Chris says. Eager to learn more about his instructor, he asks, "So how did you end up here?"

A long pause ensues, and Pierce's eyes grow distant. "I was in the Gulf War," he explains. "In the Special Air Service of the British Army, I saw death up close. That gruesome business changes you."

"Okay … but I've never heard of that group."

"You might be more familiar with their US counterpart. They're known as Special Forces."

"Yes, I've heard of them."

"Anyway, when I returned home, it took some adjustment to civilian life. Unfortunately my marriage failed, and now I enjoy the freedom of doing as I please. But doing so causes unimaginable loneliness. To counteract that, I teach my students this form of combat."

Quickly possible responses sift through Chris's mind. But he doesn't know what to say. Finally Chris says, "I'm sorry things worked out the way they did."

"Many thanks," Pierce says, who motions toward the palisade. "I sold most of my possessions, and I live on a boat where I fish a lot. It's moored to a dock far from the longbow targets along the lakeshore. I'm sure if you ventured there, you'd be able to see the craft."

"I doubt I'll have the chance to see it with all my training for the tournament," Chris says.

"Right," Pierce says, nodding.

"But how did you become an expert?" Chris plumbs, not quite following Pierce's history.

"In the Special Air Service, all modern weapons were at my disposal. But I have always been keen on using cutting instruments, such as daggers, which spurred my interest in long swords. When my active duty ended, I had enough savings and plenty of time to wield that medieval weapon at an accelerated pace. I trained for several years to reach the level where I could teach it."

"Oh."

"And your chances of winning the tournament will improve if you are wearing a suit of armor. Do you have any?"

"No," Chris says flatly.

"Then you should be able to find an armor shop along Ye Olde Artisans," Pierce suggests. "It's best if you go straightaway so that I can test your offensive and defensive skills later on today when you are fully armored, not at the end of the day when it will be too late."

"Okay," Chris says.

"To look like a knight on your return trip," Pierce says, "you'll need to carry your weapon—one that you'll be using in today's tournament." He hands Chris a padded long sword from the table.

"All right," Chris says. "It looks too big to be sheathed."

"Good observation since it's padded," Pierce says. "That's why you'll have to carry it until you're wearing armor."

"I'll manage," Chris says with an air of confidence, and then he heads back to the fair.

"See you in a while!" Pierce hollers.

With a brief wave of his hand and turn of his head, Chris says, "See you later."

The day, which started so horrendously with his scrubbed mission, holds new possibilities for Chris, for he had slain an old fear—speaking to the crowd. Being a challenger in today's tournament would have been unimaginable to him ever since being knocked unconscious in his youth. Moreover, the possibility of changing careers hopefully in five to ten years intrigues him as well.

Again he heads through the forest. But along the way he stops where the path abuts a nearby stream.

Amid a cathedral of trees where shafts of golden sunlight pierce the canopy and spotlight leaf-choked earth a queen fairy towers above her flock of kids, their faces painted and backs winged, as they run hither and thither with abandon. Eventually his presence draws their attention.

She approaches him slowly. Ethereal in a sheer white gown, her long blonde hair flowing over it, she clutches a silver wand and wears a golden crown. When the two meet, she asks in a blithe English voice, "Why are you in such a hurry? Take a break from the rigors of your day. Relax in nature's splendor, for it is sublime. Her rolling mountains, pristine lake, majestic trees, and cobalt-blue sky—those elements beckon you to capture their image somehow. Indeed, it reminds me of something I overheard a painter in the forest once say, one who was trying to do just that," she says, motioning to the landscape around her. "Over all, rocks, wood, and water, brooded the spirit of repose, and the silent energy of nature stirred the soul to its inmost depths."[32]

Chris stands with his mouth agape, eyes wide, and brow crinkled, dumbfounded. Coming to his senses, he ventures, "I think you've overestimated my artistic ability. Actually I am a man of science who needs to find a blacksmith. Do you know where I can locate one?"

"The realm of swords and armor—it's so primitive," she says. "Providence is the domain for you, one that cannot be explained— serendipity, synchronicity, coincidences, kismet, luck."

"But the wizard told me that providence isn't such a good thing," Chris says.

"That sounds just like something that the old goat would say," she says as she wrinkles her nose. "But the difference between us is that I bestow one-time gifts of fortune whereas he creates these magical objects of a permanent nature. Then he expresses surprise— surprise—when things go awry!"

"What do you mean?"

"Oh, one day many years ago the two of us crossed paths. Apparently he had fashioned a talisman that pointed in the direction of the closest cache of precious stones—either lying in the shallow ground or in someone's possession or dwelling. He said he gave it to a leper out of pity. One day when the recipient was foraging for food or perhaps seeking buried treasure, he was ambushed. Some pillagers robbed him of his precious possession and then went on to sack the surrounding shires. When word got back to the wizard, he figured that their riches would grow inexorably, creating a rival army so vast that it could not be stopped. In his search to find the villains, he and his armed entourage happened upon us, talked to me for a short while, and then continued on."

"I see why he won't bestow any magic upon me because he told a similar story earlier today," Chris says, his eyes sparkling from gaining insight into the wizard's life, especially a secondhand story about the sage. But it's yet another far-fetched anecdote. No doubt the two of them are relishing their roles, he assumes.

"I hear that he doesn't bestow magic upon *anyone* anymore," she corrects. "No doubt my rival has a dim view of me. But what fun would the world be without providence smiling upon someone once in a while?"

"A dull place indeed," Chris says. "So what charms do you have for me?"

Placing her left hand on her hip, she admonishes, "Some folk want their luck buttered."[33] Swiftly regaining her composure, she adds, "It doesn't work if you *expect* your luck to change, but I have been known to sprinkle good fortune on *others*." As she turns aside, the palm of her hand extending toward the fair, her outstretched translucent wings are revealed. "But someday, good fortune could happen to you," she says softly. "Things which you do not hope happen more frequently than things which you do hope."[34]

"As luck would have it, I'm in a tournament whose winner will become a knight later on today," Chris says, hopeful that he can gain an edge in the event. Thinking better of his remark, he adds, "That's very generous of you to invite me to join your group. But I need to make the most of today, which includes training for the tournament."

"You're not interested then?" she asks. "The enchanted forest awaits you. You will find that there is more to life than wielding a long sword and seeking the protection of a castle."

Playing along, Chris says, "Maybe in another life, but thanks anyway. I really must get going. See you later."

"Good-bye," she says with a tinge of sadness.

With haste, Chris marches off.

Like the waxing sun, Chris's spirits climb higher as he makes his way back to the fair until he spots the jester in front of the courtyard gate.

His face grimacing with contempt, the jester hisses, "Have you quit yet?"

"Of course not!" Chris says.

Accosting Chris, the jester taunts, "You're so bad. I could beat you in ten moves!"

"We'll see about that!" Chris snorts, buoyed by his nascent confidence.

"A fight then using our padded long swords?" the jester asks.

"You betcha!" Chris says.

"When?"

"At noon."

"Good! I will see you then at the Combat Arena, halfling!"

CHAPTER 8

ARMOR MAKES THE MAN

The warm sunlight dims and gradually surrenders to a blanket of high clouds, for to the west darkness grows.

Heading northward along a serpentine path from the courtyard, Chris threads his way through the hordes of people and arrives at the broad expanse of Ye Olde Artisans, a collection of guilder shops bordering an oval path—a richly colored woodworking stand, an iridescent glass store, a stately jewelry building, and a cottage brimming with artwork, some of which are displayed outdoors and depict nature in dramatic rendition.

For an instant a flare of blue light draws Chris's attention out of the corner of his eye. Various wares dangling in front of Ye Olde Glass Shoppe twist in the breeze.

To satisfy his curiosity, he heads that way. Upon entering the store, he spots a relic in the corner—an antique telescope.

Chris is drawn to the long, thin tube perched on its stand. He inspects the crude instrument and then lays his weapon on the floor. He crouches and then peers through the eyepiece.

* * *

When he gazed through the twenty-inch window on the space station's floor earlier, Chris discovered that the Himalayas were cloaked by storms. In fact, his sister had tried and failed to reach the summit of the world's tallest mountain. Like so many others who had tried before her, she fell short of her goal and remains bitter about it to this day.

More than fifty years have passed since vaunted explorers Sir Edmund Hillary from New Zealand and his Sherpa guide, Tenzing Norgay, successfully scaled Mt. Everest, whose zenith can be reached during a two-week window during mid-May and then a few days between early September through late November, weather permitting.

It has been written that "climbing a high mountain may be modern man's outlet for the classic hero's struggle codified by Joseph Campbell: approaching, confronting, and then overcoming the weaknesses and demons that haunt us and obstruct us."[35]

Almost piercing the stratosphere, Mt. Everest poses a gauntlet of perilous challenges, preventing all but a few climbers from ever reaching the apex each year—deadly and demanding terrain, low oxygen levels, fierce winds, and extremely cold temperatures. Death from above can swiftly snuff out life in the form of avalanches that cause the greatest fatalities.

Also arrayed against mountaineers are a multitude of health problems, including mountain sickness (headaches, insomnia, and coughing fits), illness (fever, dysentery, and cerebral edema, a swelling of the brain), and dehydration from sweating and exhalation. A loss of appetite and an inefficient digestive system force the body to consume its muscle mass as an alternate energy source. Further demoralizing climbers is the occasional sight of a corpse along the trail, one of close to two hundred claimed by the mountain.

Unlike ice floes that tumble into an adjacent body of water, Everest's landlocked Khumbu Glacier breaks up as it nears the lower reaches of the snow line called the Khumbu Ice Fall just above base camp at an altitude of 17,600 feet, fracturing into turquoise ice blocks—some of which are the size of an apartment building and weigh up to thirty tons—that could move without warning. Between the ice blocks are gaps that are called crevasses, and these have claimed at least nineteen lives. And sheer drops near the pinnacle invite a spectacular demise—knifelike ridges with a seven-thousand-foot fall on one side and a ten-thousand-foot precipice on the other.

To reach the summit, mountaineers must ascend above twenty-six thousand feet, an altitude above which acclimatization—a time-consuming process of adapting to a higher elevation without causing mountain sickness or death—is impossible. Accordingly, the height above that altitude is called the death zone because climbers can only live above that elevation for a few days before they expire from an insufficient atmosphere.

So high is the world's tallest peak that the oxygen level is 30 percent that of sea level. Some mountaineers may hallucinate because of hypoxia, an inadequate level of oxygen in the bloodstream. Brain cells die by the minute. Heart rates double or triple to compensate for the low oxygen levels. Similarly, red blood cells multiply as part of the acclimatization process, thickening the blood and doubling the likelihood of a heart attack.

Climbers mitigate the effects of impaired judgment by using supplemental oxygen, which lowers the effective altitude by two thousand to four thousand feet at summit level, whose use was likened by David Breashears, a five-time Everest summiteer, as "running on a treadmill and breathing through a straw."[36]

Many other dangers lurk, adding to mountaineers' woes. Ferocious storms that produce whiteout conditions make it very difficult or impossible for climbers to find their tents. Another concern for mountaineers is the jet stream—a river of hurricane-force winds circling Earth at an altitude of six miles—that has been known to descend a few thousand feet, slamming into and raking the mountain with winds in excess of one hundred miles per hour, sweeping unsheltered climbers to their deaths.

A final danger is that prolonged exposure to extremely cold temperatures can lead to frostbite or worse, hypothermia that can be fatal.

Most mountaineers and their guides typically spend about a month on the mountain—in part due to acclimatization and stocking camps with supplies. Near the end of their trip, most climbers begin their ascent to the pinnacle around midnight, where temperatures hover between minus ten to minus twenty degrees. Although the apex looms about three thousand vertical feet above them and spans a walking distance of a mile and a half—a veritable high-altitude marathon—mountaineers wearing headlamps plod along at twelve feet per minute. Their slow pace is due to the thin atmosphere, steep grade, and knee- to thigh-deep snow. Since temperature decreases with height, climbers face the coldest temperatures during their highest and longest trip away from camp—eighteen hours to summit and back.

But reaching the top is only half the journey; the descent has proven far deadlier.

For every five mountaineers who reach Everest's peak, one will die on the return trip due to exhaustion, exposure, or falls. Some climbers succumb to summit fever, in which their at-all-costs strategy to reach the top leaves no reserve for the return trip. Others die from exhausting their supplemental oxygen supply. Such tragedies range from simple mismanagement of their oxygen canisters to bottleneck delays along ridges and outcroppings as other expeditions take advantage of the short climbing window in which to mount their summit charge and then retreat from the death zone. Reducing the fatality rate, however, is a mandatory turnaround time of two or three in the afternoon, regardless of whether mountaineers have reached the top.

Historically the mountain exacts an overall 10 percent fatality rate, paradoxically increasing the mountain's lure.

Evaluating the obstacles arrayed against climbers, Chris says to himself, "You can't summit Mount Everest anytime you feel like it."

Chris remembers an early training tape about the working conditions inside the space station—a temperature-controlled seventy-two-degree, sea level–pressurized interior providing an atmosphere that allows for normal cognitive functions, a dining area in which to eat microwaveable foods in complete comfort, and a sleeping area in which crew members can slumber in any position they want, even upside down!

While astronauts have a lower fatality rate than that of climbers, space flight is inherently dangerous.

* * *

After he finds the telescope's optics dusty, he tracks down the shopkeeper and says, "Excuse me. I am interested in this telescope. Do you have something to clean the dust off the lens with? I'd like to see if it works."

The shopkeeper's head is adorned by a kerchief, below which a tendril of dark brown hair escapes. Her left eye is hidden by a cornflower blue eye patch, and her frame is bedecked by a matching colored, sleeveless surcoat over a white tunic. "Give me a minute to find one," she says with an English timbre. Immediately she retreats to the rear of the store and returns with a white cloth. While slowly cleaning the front lens, the shopkeeper inquires, "Why are you interested in the movement of the stars?"

Sensing a shared interest, Chris says, "Oh, that's a long story," not wanting to explain his childhood issues. "In any event, I'm an astronaut. I was a member of the shuttle crew that unexpectedly landed at Edwards Air Force Base this morning. But I didn't have a chance to deploy my experiment because my mission was cut short. So I'm here for a few hours to enjoy the day until my return flight tomorrow."

"I, too, wanted to be an astronaut," she says, "but that was a long time ago."

"What happened?" Chris asks.

"Oh, an accident when I was young," she explains. "My friends were playing with firecrackers, and one headed in my direction. It exploded close to my face, and I was blinded in my left eye. Since my parents racked up huge debts to pay for all my operations, I needed to repay them by getting a job as soon as possible and giving up my chance to attend university. As a result, I had no shot at becoming an astronaut."

"I'm so sorry," Chris says. "That's a tragedy."

She beckons Chris over to the eyepiece and says, "In any event, I'm jealous. Very few people get to venture into space. I'll bet you saw a lot of things that most of us will never see."

Chris walks over to the telescope and angles it toward the window. He stoops, craning his neck to peer through the eyepiece. To his amazement, the instrument functions normally despite its ancient age. But the clouds above are not the canvas he's looking for. Slowly he stands upright, looks at the shopkeeper, and then says, "Well, yes. The view was incredible! It gave me a new perspective of life on Earth. Flying across a module was a blast. In fact, I felt like a kid again."

Looking out the window, the shopkeeper says, "You joined an exclusive club of those who have been in space and looked at the world in wonder. When you arrived here today, what caught your attention?"

"Oh ... the mountains, the lake, the huge trees, and fresh air."

"Typical of any alpine setting. What else?"

After mulling it over, Chris mutters, "It was such a big blur."

"Perhaps you weren't focused on distant objects," the shopkeeper says, returning her gaze back to him. "Maybe what held your attention was right in front of you. Tell me. When you traveled here today, how many blue cars did you see?"

"I have no idea," Chris says, shrugging.

"I would imagine quite a few," the shopkeeper muses. "Perhaps you can answer this. What image is on the back of a ten-dollar bill, and what is printed on the other side of a one-dollar bill directly opposite George Washington's portrait?"

"I don't know," Chris snarls, stumped and annoyed at this line of questioning. "It's not important to me."

"Just because it's unimportant to you doesn't mean those images don't exist," the shopkeeper says. Gesturing to the window, she adds, "Don't you find it odd that there are objects and even opportunities in plain sight—they can be natural or man-made, stationary or in motion, made of steel or malleable such as currency—and yet their presence, image, or details completely elude you?" Shaking her head, she adds, "People only see what they are prepared to see."[37]

"Why should I care?" Chris asks, folding his arms. "I don't think anyone will pass fake one-dollar bills. Also, I suppose denominations of twenty dollars and higher are the ones most likely to be counterfeited."

"Then perhaps profiting from opportunities that are visible to everyone but discerned by a few would interest you."

"Like what?"

"Let's see," the shopkeeper says, looking around at her artwork. "Got it. How about maps? You probably see a national or state map every day. Are they important to you?"

"Only if it concerns weather or driving directions."

Motioning to the rest of her wares, she says, "Perhaps if you look more closely at the various pieces of artwork for sale, the answer might come to you."

"Sorry, I don't have the time."

"All right then. If I had shown you one of the mosaics in the store, then the answer would have been obvious. Did you ever realize that there was a story behind the shape of each state?"

Chris pauses for a moment and then admits, "Not until you just mentioned it."

"Then you lost out on your chance to make a lot of money," the shopkeeper says.

"If that was apparent to you, then perhaps you took advantage of it."

"No, someone else beat me to it, and I'm sure his fortunes were rewarded accordingly."

Nodding, Chris says, "I guess I'll have to find ways to develop a keen eye for spotting opportunities in the future. Hopefully I'll profit from them. But right now I'm pressed for time, and I need to obtain a suit of armor. Do you know where I can find a blacksmith because I was selected to be in a contest whose champion will become a knight?"

"Just go out the door, and it's three shops to your right," the proprietor suggests, pointing that way. "Good luck!"

"Thank you," Chris says, and then he retrieves his weapon, shakes her hand, and heads outside.

A roof of white clouds creeps lower in the sky, filtering the sun and cooling off the day.

Returning to the lane, Chris presses on until a familiar tune interrupts his quest. Looking down and then retrieving his cell phone, Chris says, "Hello."

"Hi, it's Andrew. Are you still training?"

"Not at this instant," Chris says, resting the tip of his weapon on the ground. "But I'm still on track to compete in today's tournament. In fact, I'm on my way to a blacksmith's shop right now. Have you enjoyed the day so far?"

"Yeah, I've had fun," Andrew says. "In fact, it's been hard to have such a good time while knowing that you've been breaking a sweat for hours. If I'd known beforehand that I was sending you to a hard-labor camp, then I probably would have suggested something else."

"I've been really busy," Chris says, ignoring the barb. "What have you been up to?"

"Oh, I just watched a play over at the Globe Theater," Andrew says. "Then I went window shopping in countless stores. I'll probably buy some scenic prints late this afternoon so I won't have to drag them around for the rest of the day. So, how is your training going?"

"It's been a frustrating—"

"Then why are you still training?" Andrew intones.

"There's a lot for me to learn in a short period of time," Chris says, sensing where this conversation is headed, "which is true for anyone trying to learn a new sport in a day."

"All right," Andrew says. "Why expend so much effort on a silly tournament?"

"I'm worried that I won't have a second chance to deploy my payload," Chris says. "I've heard rumors that NASA will end the payload specialist position next year. Is there any truth to that?"

"It's not official yet," Andrew says, "but that's what I've heard from my friends."

"Then yesterday was my first and last trip to space," Chris says, his eyes downcast.

"I'm sorry," Andrew says. "I didn't want to tell you earlier because it would have made a bad day worse. But your payload would still make it to the space station, and you would get all the credit. Instead a mission specialist would deploy what you've designed."

"Good for him."

"So, how is your training for this tournament helping you?"

"Today's mission was the pinnacle of my career. Because I won't have a second chance to deploy my payload, it puts a whole new perspective on my current job. Since I've just experienced a huge setback—"

"What's this talk about a huge setback? I just told you that someone else would deliver *your* payload to the space station. Where you've succeeded before in designing a payload, you can succeed again. NASA will not stop delivering payloads to the space station just because your position no longer exists. So where's the setback?"

Chris sighs and then says, "A major loss of face."

"So your pride is wounded," Andrew says. "Is that it?"

"Yeah ... that's about it," Chris admits. "But I've found some friends to help me with some childhood issues that might lead me to another career."

"What's that?"

"Pursuing the martial arts."

"I suppose we'll have a lot of time to talk about that on the trip back. But I've found that my fellow retired astronauts tend to be consultants to NASA contractors. I'm sure you can leverage your experience accordingly. You don't want to throw that all away."

"But I don't have the experience in space that you do."

"We have all reached our positions in life by being committed to our profession. Don't give up so easily."

"Like you said, we'll have plenty of time to discuss this on the trip back. If you want to see me in action, I'm supposed to fight the jester at noon at the Combat Arena."

"Maybe I'll drop by and see your progress."

"Okay, well, I've got to go."

"See you then."

* * *

Back on the street Chris threads his way through the crowd until he eyes a gleaming set of armor in a blacksmith's shop window. The sign above the entrance reads, "Invincible Armor." Hopeful, the apprentice rushes inside where he sees a burly blacksmith garbed in a linen-colored tunic and a brown apron. His forehead beads with sweat, and his eyes reflect the nearby firelight. In his right hand, the guildsman wields a hammer that flattens a nearly finished incandescent metal blade—which he clutches with his gloved left hand—upon an anvil. The luminescence slowly fades with every strike of his tool until he quenches the blade in a bucket of water and then lays it on a counter. Next to him is a tray-sized bed of fire fed by soft coal, and above it, there's a large circular flue.

"Excuse me," Chris says, sensing his opportunity. "I'd like to get some armor."

Looking at and then approaching him, the blacksmith rasps in an English accent, "Sure. I could use more business. How much armor do you need?"

"A full set," Chris says. "By the way, the armor displayed out front is very impressive, but it looks too big for me."

"I put the largest set on display to attract the most people," the blacksmith boasts. He stops an arm's length away from his patron. "You should see all the visitors standing there, gawking at it. Anyway, let me take a look at you." Scanning Chris from head to toe, the tradesman adds, "Got it. By the way, what's the occasion?"

"I am in a tournament whose victor will be knighted late this afternoon," Chris says. He places his padded long sword on a nearby table and likewise empties his pockets.

"Good luck to you!" the blacksmith says as he wipes his brow with his sleeve. "Have you ever fought before?"

"No. That's why I have someone training me how to fight."

"Really? Who?"

"Pierce."

With a slight nod, the blacksmith says, "He'll certainly show you the moves." As the tradesman lumbers to the back room, he adds, "Now give me a few minutes to gather your armor." After making several trips to retrieve Chris's equipment from the back room and place the materials on the shop floor, the blacksmith eventually brings out the last piece, a helmet, and lays it on the table.

"Before I forget, let me give you this letter that was given to me," Chris says as he retrieves his missive from the table and gives it to the tradesman.

"Thank you," the blacksmith says. He inspects the envelope intently. "You have friends in high places," he adds, pointing to the royal wax seal. The tradesman hastily opens the letter and reads aloud, "The bearer shall receive a full set of armor ... gratis." Looking at Chris, the blacksmith says, "You are fortunate indeed. Since you've never fought before, you don't know how to put on armor, so I'll help you."

Chris dons armor for several minutes until he is virtually covered from head to toe in a steel skin. He has chain mail draped around his neck, lining the gap in the armor between his torso and his upper arms, not to mention between his upper legs and groin. A stretch here, a walk there, and he is satisfied with his metallic shell. Standing on the far side of the room, Chris opens his helmet's visor and says, "No complaints here."

"Good," the tradesman says. Grabbing a belt and securing it around Chris's waist, the blacksmith adds, "Just give me a few seconds to attach your weapon to your belt's ring so that you won't have to carry it for the rest of the day." The merchant wrestles the two together and then says, "There. You're all finished."

"Thanks," Chris says. "You know, if I won the tournament, it would be a dream come true. But I probably won't win because strength has never been my forte."

"Fortunately strength is not the sole factor in wielding a long sword," the blacksmith says. He grabs a pitcher from the table, pours himself a glass of water, and quaffs it. Wiping his mouth with the back of his hand, he adds, "Stamina, agility, guile, and quickness help too. Speaking of dreams, my aspiration was to start my own armor shop. I knew that in order to make my dream come true, it was going to require more resources than I had. Before I went to the bank, I followed my father's advice. 'No man is wise enough by himself.'[38] So ... one of my friends builds small boats for a living. Sure, it's not shaping steel, but being a business owner is the same— work on your own, toil more hours, assume more risk. He made sure that this was not only something I wanted to do but also that I had a plan for carrying it out, in which case the bank would be more likely to approve my loan. Fortunately that's what happened."

"That's impressive," Chris says as he doffs his helmet and lays it on the table. "But I need to master a new craft first before I take the plunge."

"Of course," the blacksmith says. "Just as a network of friends helped me, the same principle applies to you. I'm sure you can make new friends by joining a guild, club, or association. Perhaps you saw the guilds as you entered Ye Olde Artisans? As far as clubs are concerned, most are held during festival hours, like games of skill, such as axe and dart throwing and the lot."

"Although I did try archery briefly, I didn't see any of the clubs you mentioned. I haven't been everywhere just yet. Since today is the last day of the fair, I'm very pressed for time. I need to learn how to wield my weapon," Chris says, grasping his padded long sword by the handle.

"Yes, you're right," the blacksmith agrees. Gesturing to the pitcher, he asks, "By the way, would you like anything to drink?"

"No, thanks," Chris says.

The blacksmith pours himself another glass of water and gulps it down with gusto. "Perhaps other clubs' activities that might interest you take place after the hordes have left. One such group is the Tall Tales Club. Have you ever heard of it?"

"No," Chris says, shaking his head.

"Regardless," the blacksmith says, "once you're a member of any guild, club, or association, that group's culture allows you a chance to make mistakes, and your fellow members can offer constructive ways to improve. In fact, should you belong to the Tall Tales Club, if your attempts to regale them fall flat, the experience stays within the group without any consequences carrying over outside the organization. So you have nothing to lose and everything to gain by joining one."

"Really?" Chris says, still skeptical.

"In this world a man must either be anvil or hammer,"[39] the blacksmith says, pointing to the tools of his trade with pride. "Indeed, perhaps the best example of striking a note for change is persuading the crowd to advance your cause. That's why joining such a club should be important to you because it allows you to improve your technique."

"I see your point," Chris says, nodding. "Now that you mention it, had I been a member of the Tall Tales Club, I would have received advice from acquaintances who have nothing to gain, not total strangers like the one who advised me this morning. He had an ulterior motive, and now I'm dealing with the consequences."

"That's too bad," the blacksmith says.

"Is the jester a member?" Chris scoffs.

"Fortunately not," the blacksmith says.

"Good," Chris says with a subtle nod. "But I did receive some suggestions on how to improve my speech today."

"Really? From the stranger?"

"Yes. His name is James."

"Who is he?"

"He used to be a jester, but the king retired him in favor of the current one."

"That's too bad," the blacksmith says and wipes perspiration off his forehead with the back of his hand. "That's why you should own your own business. No one else can sack you! Maybe the fool just got into a rut, and the king tired of the same old jokes, the same wacky routines," the tradesman says and then mimics a jester's broad grin. "Possibly James didn't take the time to improve his calling."

"Maybe," Chris says with a snicker.

"Another reason why you might consider owning your own business is that you are not making someone else rich off your efforts. Instead your hard work goes toward the bottom line of your company."

"It all sounds appealing."

"In fact," the blacksmith says, "almost without exception, there is only one way to make a great deal of money in the business world—and that is in one's own business. The man who wants to go into business for himself should choose a field which he knows and understands."[40]

"You make it sound like it's a license to print money," Chris sniffs.

"Of course," the blacksmith says, "not all businesses are profitable. Seeking the highest reward also exposes you to the greatest risk. That challenge is not for the fainthearted. In fact, most businesses go under even during the best of times. That's why a prospective business owner must understand the competitive landscape before such undertakings."

"My interest is in the martial arts," Chris says, "and if I become a kung fu master, *then* I'll look to a bank to help me own my own business—a school where I can train my students how to defend themselves."

"Good," the blacksmith says.

"In any event," Chris says, "I need to get going."

"By the way," the blacksmith says, "don't forget your sneakers."

"Thanks for reminding me," Chris says. He retrieves his helmet and collects the rest of his belongings.

"I don't remember hearing a horse outside," the blacksmith says, glancing at the door. "If you're on foot, then you should change back into your sneakers so that you don't get blisters, and you can make better time than walking in your armored shoes."

"Oh, good idea," Chris says. "Thanks. I'll do that outside. I'm sure you have other pressing activities." Taking a step closer, he adds, "Nice to meet you," as he shakes the tradesman's hand.

"It was a pleasure meeting you," the blacksmith says, "and good luck with the tournament!"

"Thanks," Chris says as he heads outdoors.

* * *

It doesn't take long for passersby to cast strange looks at Chris since he's horseless, in armor, wearing sneakers, and carrying his own helmet that holds his armored shoes, wallet, and cell phone.

For a short while Chris follows the path to the southeast, which then snakes to the west until he reaches the Combat Arena, where the jester, already in armor, is waiting for him. The sole occupant in the stands is Andrew, Chris assumes.

"You'll find that your weapon is a lot duller than your mouth," Chris taunts as he replaces his shoes. He subsequently dons his helmet, closes his visor, and readies his padded long sword.

"If you think your armor is going to protect you," the jester says, pointing his weapon at his adversary, "you're a lot more fragile than you think!"

The jester and Chris circle each other, with the latter pointing his weapon diagonally behind him. Suddenly the jester charges Chris, who swings at his opponent's midsection only to have it parried. Moving closer still, the jester manages to bind Chris's weapon and grabs it with his other hand in quick succession, momentarily focusing the apprentice's attention on his own padded long sword. The jester quickly slips his leg behind Chris's. And with one push with his right elbow, the jester knocks Chris to the ground, creating a large cloud of dust.

Looming over and pointing his weapon at Chris, the jester chortles, "It's about time your aspirations came crashing down to earth! How many times do I have to tell you that you'll never be a knight? Your dismal performance will provide me with even more fodder to entertain the crowds today!" He leaves triumphantly.

Defeated and upset, Chris removes his helmet and hurls it to the ground. Slowly he returns to his feet. Hopping around on one foot and then his other, he removes his foot armor and tosses them to the ground for good measure. Feeling the world collapsing around him, Chris slumps to the ground and covers his eyes with his gauntlets—armored gloves. What seemed like a promising day under the wizard and Pierce's tutelage dissolves into bitter disappointment in an instant. *Can I do anything right?* Chris wonders.

"It's been a tough day for you," a familiar voice calls out.

His heart filled with rage, his nostrils flaring, Chris snaps, "I quit!" He turns around and faces Andrew, who approaches him. "Apparently I'm no good at this," the apprentice says, "and I'm not much of an astronaut either!"

"Do you think that I learned it all on my first try?" Andrew asks and draws up to the deflated one.

"Things worked out for you, didn't they?" Chris says with a petulant scowl.

"I took my lumps just like everyone else," Andrew says with his hands on his hips. "It took years of hard work, and today you've persevered for only a few hours. That's not commitment!"

Upon further reflection Chris nods his head. "I suppose you're right." Apparently his self-pity and low sense of self-worth got the better of him. Andrew is certainly correct about commitment, and that logic prevents Chris from calling it a day. But what does Andrew know about fighting with long swords? Wouldn't Andrew have been just as deeply disappointed during his NASA days if someone with inferior credentials as an astronaut had been selected for the next mission instead of him? Still awash in uncertainties and seeking answers, Chris thanks Andrew, dons his sneakers, collects the rest of the objects of his wrath, and heads west to see the wizard.

* * *

Chris bursts into the sage's fire-lit chamber, where the hiss of the fire matches his mood. He hastily deposits his helmet on the floor. Turning toward the silhouetted one, Chris, whose face is covered with a fine layer of dirt, says, "The jester beat me in just ten moves. It was so depressing that I told a friend that I quit. Fortunately he talked me out of it."

"Good for your friend," the wizard says, apparently still reading his tome. "Regarding the jester, he isn't even in the tournament."

"If I can't defeat him," Chris says, wiping dirt off his cheek, "then who can I beat? Obviously I can't beat anyone!"

"There is nothing either good or bad, but thinking makes it so,"[41] the wizard says.

"The bad news is that after hours of training," Chris mutters, "I lost to someone in just ten moves."

"You are not a failure," the wizard says. "It is just that the outcome was unsuccessful."

"But I still lost!" Chris says as a pang of hopelessness wells up inside of him. "It all feels the same to me."

Closing his book and looking at Chris, the wizard says in a slow but reassuring voice, "Nobody likes to lose, but you think that you will continue to do so." The sage walks around the lectern and crosses the floor. "Now let me get some candles so that we can talk about this in a civilized manner. I wasn't expecting to see you at this hour."

"Sorry for barging in," Chris says, running his gauntlet through his hair, still stunned from the quick turn of events. "But what you just said is correct. I expect to keep losing in light of what just happened to me."

The wizard retrieves a pair of white pillar candles from a closet and then draws up to the fireplace, where he lights both of them. "Perhaps your attempt to defeat the jester was not all in vain," he says and then turns around carefully and proceeds to the lectern. "We learn wisdom from failure much more than from success. We often discover what will do, by finding out what will not do; and probably he who never made a mistake never made a discovery."[42]

"Okay," Chris says, his voice trailing off. "So what do I need to do?"

Placing the candles on the candlestick holders, which branch from the base and flank the lectern, the wizard asks, "Remember I told you that you had to enter the land of failure to get what you want?"

"Yes," Chris says. He notices that the candlelight casts unflattering shadows on the wizard's wizened and pleated face.

"Then accept failure as part of life," the sage says.

"How do I do that?" Chris asks, cringing at the thought.

"Have you ever heard of alchemy?" the wizard asks.

"Yes," Chris says. "I think it has something to do with turning metal into gold. But I don't really see what that has to do with me."

"The craft calls for failure not just some of the time, not just most of the time, but just about all the time," the wizard says, "until you make a breakthrough several months, years, or decades hence. The practice of the art will not allow your first failure to become an excuse to give up. Persevering in alchemy is all about the process, and failure is ingrained into the process!"

"What you just described was man versus nature," Chris says, shaking his head. "What advice do you have about dealing with people? As I mentioned before, I got knocked out as a kid, and just a few minutes ago the jester defeated me."

"Failure is not you enemy," the wizard says. "Failure is your friend, provided that you learn from your missteps."

"Why does that always sounds better when it happens to someone else?" Chris asks, glancing away. "I never enjoy failure."

"Look, I cannot change your past, but I can change the lens through which you view the error of your ways," the wizard says. "Experience is the name everyone gives to their mistakes."[43]

The fireplace pops in the background, momentarily diverting Chris's attention. "So I guess Pierce would tell me what I am doing wrong and how to fix it," the apprentice ventures.

"Exactly!" the wizard says. "The jester exposed a weakness that Pierce will be able to remedy. Besides, I think you have underestimated the fool. He doesn't spend all his time making everyone feel three feet tall," the sage adds, pointing to his right just so high.

"So he has practiced!" Chris says.

"Let's just say he has had a lot of time on his hands to sharpen his swordplay," the wizard hints, "which brings up another subject. The jester varies his approach."

"Doesn't everyone?" Chris chafes.

"What happens if you no longer react to criticisms?" the wizard asks. "Then the jester is out of luck. So he varies his approach. When his taunts didn't work, he defeated and initially daunted you. Once he finds out that he ultimately failed yet again, expect him to change his approach accordingly. That is precisely what I expect *you* to do as well. Change your approach if what you are trying to do isn't working!"

Chris nods.

"Likewise, that begs another question," the wizard says. He walks around the lectern and stops an arm's length away from Chris.

"Who are you comparing yourself to, and is that reason enough to quit?"

"I compared myself to the jester," Chris says.

"And?" the wizard says, his voice rising.

"When I clashed with the giant," Chris says, "you told me that I incorrectly compared myself to others."

"Right ... and?" the wizard says, motioning his hand in a circular fashion to his student.

"If I can't compare myself to others," Chris says, scratching his head with his gauntlet, "then I would imagine the only choice left is some sort of comparison to what I've done earlier today."

"Right."

"What I should have done is considered whether I improved myself over the course of the morning, which I did. So there's no reason to quit."

"I couldn't have said it better myself," the wizard says in a matter-of-fact voice.

"But the jester is such a pain," Chris says, his arms outstretched. "I'm sure I would be a lot more successful if he were not here. Can't you make him go away?" he asks jokingly. Upon reflection the apprentice adds, "He's making my day miserable."

"You'll find that adversity in life makes one better," the wizard says.

"But I'm not looking forward to more adversity *today*," Chris says, reflecting on the day's unexpected turn of events.

"Do you think you'd actually improve if you were battling a blind competitor?"

"Of course not," Chris says.

"Then look forward to competing against someone who can challenge you," the wizard says, pointing at Chris. "What we obtain too cheap, we esteem too lightly; it is dearness only that gives everything its value."[44]

"But I still don't like the jester."

"Do you think he's your harshest critic?"

"Absolutely."

"Judging by the number of times you have tried to quit today, I'd say that you are your harshest critic," the wizard says, stroking his beard. "Our greatest foes, and whom we must chiefly combat, are within."[45]

"Well," Chris murmurs, "I suppose you're right."

"Now, getting back to the jester," the wizard says, "he only answers to the king, who would be furious if his favorite entertainer were no longer here. So I am sorry. You will have to live with him. Besides, if he weren't giving you a hard time, I'm sure someone else would."

"All right," Chris says, resigned to the fact.

"Enough about the jester and his ilk," the wizard says, waving his hand dismissively. "Remember when I told you that you should see the juggler today?"

"Yes," Chris says.

"I think now is a good time," the wizard says as he nods his head slowly. "Perhaps this diversion will help clear your mind. Her shop is in the courtyard."

"But should I see her before or after lunch because the king invited the contestants to the castle for lunch at one?" Chris inquires as he retrieves his helmet off the floor.

"Before lunch."

"Okay," Chris says, whose composure rapidly changes to one of concern. "When will I see you next?"

"Since you've already quit twice from encounters with the jester today," the wizard says, "I'll see you when you least expect it."

Caught off guard, Chris says, "Oh ... whatever. Anyway, thanks for your advice, and I'll see you when I least expect it, whenever that is." And he takes his leave.

His hopes buoyed, Chris heads outside, for the tide had turned yet again for the apprentice. Perhaps he could salvage something from this day—something that could last a lifetime.

* * *

On the right side of the courtyard entrance stands the juggler's store, curiously vacant. As he eyes its wares—clubs, torches, balls, and knives—a woman's voice calls out from behind him. "I see you're interested in juggling."

"Huh," Chris says, slowly turning around.

"It's never too late to learn how to juggle," the juggler says with an English lilt. "Try it."

Before he has a chance to say no, a flurry of clubs heads his way.

Upon seeing four twirling props in the air, Chris drops his helmet. His arms flailing wildly, he desperately tries to grab all of the clubs in midair but is so overwhelmed that they all crash to the ground.

The juggler places her hands on her hips and scolds, "What's the matter? Can't juggle?"

"Never tried it," Chris grumbles as he collects his errant personal effects off the ground.

Hastily she gathers her props. An effervescent woman with ruddy cheeks and short strawberry-blonde hair, she is costumed in a sleeveless deep carrot-orange surcoat over a pale white tunic. "Fortunately you came to the right place," she says. "But you are not from around here, are you?"

"No," Chris says, shaking his head. "Actually I really didn't come here to learn how to juggle. Rather, the wizard suggested that I meet you."

"Oh," the juggler says, astonished. "He did, huh? I haven't seen or heard from him in ages. In fact, the last time I saw him about ten years ago, I was part of an acrobatic troupe and took a nasty spill. The wizard was in the audience, and he was kind enough to meet me after the performance to make sure that I was okay."

"Any broken bones?"

"Thankfully not, but I decided that it would be less dangerous if I tossed something else into the air besides my own body. That's how I became a juggler. I suppose the wizard has seen my shop over at Fun, Food & Drink, but he has never stopped by to say hello."

"I'm sorry," Chris says.

"Don't worry about it," the juggler says. "Anyway, I've got time. But do you?"

"I'm attending a royal lunch at one," Chris says, glancing at his helmet on the ground, which holds his cell phone, "so I've got ten minutes."

A hint of disfavor registers on her face. The juggler says, "That's unusual—a royal lunch. Judging from your armor and weapon, it probably has to do with being a knight."

"I'm in a contest whose *winner* will be knighted," Chris explains, "and I hope to be that person."

"I didn't know the royal family was that generous," she chafes. "Do you think you've had enough time to prepare?"

"I would have preferred to have trained for more than one day," Chris says, drawing his gauntlet to his head in bewilderment. "But I am concerned about my chances of winning the tournament because I really haven't led an active lifestyle."

"Really?" the juggler says as she begins her juggling act again. "What is it that you do?"

"I'm an engineer, and I was just recently in space," Chris says, gesturing in that direction.

"Let me get this straight," the juggler says. "You're an astronaut who would like to be a knight?"

"Well ... yes!" Chris says in a fit of pique. "My mission was aborted early this morning, and here I am preparing for the competition. In fact, Pierce is helping me work on my strength and stamina."

"Is Pierce your instructor?" the juggler asks, whose head oscillates, tracking the various trajectories of her props.

"Yes," Chris says, nodding. "Anyway, I'm also trying to undo a lifetime of physical neglect."

"That's not going to be easy to change," the juggler says.

"It's that bad?" Chris asks, marveling at the spectacle.

"Indeed," the juggler says. "Nothing is stronger than habit."[46]

"Then I have my work cut out for me," Chris says despondently.

"At least you're trying to address them today," the juggler says. Maintaining her juggling act, she whips the descending clubs on her right side of her body underneath her raised right knee upward. "I'm sure you're aware that your quest to reinvent yourself will require more than a day's toil."

"Yes," Chris says, "that's obvious. I didn't plan on becoming Hercules overnight."

"Then what prevents you from leading a more active lifestyle?" she asks, standing on two feet again and adding a few behind-the-back tosses.

Chris sighs. "I work such long hours that I get home late," he laments. "After dinner I just collapse in front of the TV for the rest of the evening with my wife."

"Dost thou love life? Then do not squander time; for that's the stuff life is made of,"[47] the juggler says. "You're wasting time watching TV and hoping or praying to be someone else you aren't right now."

"That was my escape," Chris admits. "I'm not proud of it. I just wish I had better discipline to do the things I ought to do."

"Don't worry," the juggler says as she catches the rest of her clubs. She ambles over to the display rack, exchanges props, and then returns. "You can change your ways. But first, does watching television take up all your free time?"

"No," Chris says. "On weekends I try to keep my wife entertained. If time permits, I'll sneak in an hour or two of designing my own city on a computer simulation game. On Sunday nights I take a peek at the stars through my telescope."

"That sounds like there's a lot on your plate," the juggler says, lighting her torches. "Do you think you'll totally change your physique without altering your routine?"

"I'll just work it into my schedule," Chris says without concern.

"It sounds like your schedule is completely full."

"What makes you so sure I won't be able to do it?"

With the precision of a metronome, she tosses her three torches into the air one by one and asks, "When will you find time to fit it in your schedule?"

"Oh, on my days off," Chris says.

"Do you think you'll be able to totally change your form by exercising just two days a week?" the juggler asks.

"Um … probably not."

"Then consider adding a time to work out during the workweek—either very early in the morning or late at night."

Chris remains silent in thought.

Many visitors flock to the juggler, joining Chris and hemming the proprietor in front of her shop. The audience giggles and laughs.

"Looks like your schedule during the workweek is going to change," she says. "The art of being wise is the art of knowing what to overlook."[48] Then she adds, "Especially nonproductive pursuits like watching TV!"

"I realize that now," Chris says. "But I gave up having a good time today."

"That's a good start!" the juggler lauds. "Nevertheless, I'm sure that you'll agree that getting in shape will require you to exercise during the middle of the week as well."

"Yes," Chris says, resigned to the idea. "It looks like my routine will have to change."

"Good. Concerning your schedule, what do you have planned for the rest of today?"

"After I go to the royal lunch, I'll need to continue my training with Pierce again until my first match begins late this afternoon."

"It sounds like he has your whole day planned for you," the juggler says.

"That's right," Chris says.

"What about when he's not around to plan your day?" she asks, balancing the base of one torch on the crook of her nose and extending her hands, each of which grasp a flaming prop, perpendicular to her body. "Do you think you can manage your time as well as he can?"

"I don't think so. My routine will be turned upside down because I'll be focusing more on exercising. Why do you ask?"

"You can gauge how well you're using time by recording each activity for a fortnight," she says, still balancing the base of a torch on the crook of her nose, maintaining her cross-like pose and rotating her body around in a complete circle. "That's a log of your activities before and after performing your craft."

"How come?" Chris asks. "Isn't there enough to do in one day?"

"The life which is unexamined is not worth living,"[49] the juggler says, resuming her traditional juggling act. "This will help you evaluate how you spent your time rather than relying on your memory."

"All right," Chris says. "So I log what I do. What's so important about that?"

"Since time is your most important resource, how well you manage your time will dictate whether your quest results in success."

"I thought money is your most important asset," Chris says skeptically.

"The fortunes of kingdoms wax and wane," she says, "but the life span of each king is finite. Similarly, just as you are the master of your own kingdom, you need to take measures to ensure that you use your time wisely." Altering the orbits of her props, the juggler pivots laterally at her knees as she alternates tossing one torch vertically to her left and right. "Misspending a man's time is a kind of self-homicide."[50]

With a quizzical look, Chris says, "All right. I'll be sure to make better use of my time. But there's so much to do in a day, including what you just recommended. It's such a challenge."

"That's what it takes to realize your aspirations," the juggler says. "I didn't say it was going to be easy."

"I hate to cut this short," Chris says, "but it's time for me to meet the royal family for lunch. So I'd better get going."

"Best of luck with today's match," the juggler says, and then she catches her flaming props and extinguishes them quickly.

"Thanks," Chris says as he turns away and heads off toward the castle.

CHAPTER 9

A FEAST FIT FOR A KING

For a short while Chris follows the winding lane eastward until he reaches the grassy field of the King's Court and then hikes up a narrow incline leading to the castle gate. Foreboding gray corner towers that flank the entrance loom above him and are interspersed with cross-shaped archer slits from which a deadly fusillade of arrows would rain down upon enemy forces, Chris imagines. But such notions of savagery are in sharp contrast to the revelry of his fellow patrons. Waiting for him in the bailey is a stately prince who escorts Chris to the far side of the premises. As they draw up to a building, the aromas of cooked onions and baked carrots and lamb waft from the doorway, and festive music fills the air.

The prince motions Chris inside, where a troupe of minstrels in a far corner plays jovial tunes. He hands his helmet and weapon to an attendant who then carries them into a back room. Determined to enjoy a brief respite from the drudgery of practically an all-day lesson, Chris strolls across the chamber to join the king, who is surrounded by a circle of royalty and fellow contenders.

To Chris's dismay, the crowd effectively blocks his view of the sovereign. But the monarch's voice still registers a familiar tone. The crown eventually suggests that everyone join him for lunch. Slowly the crowd disperses. As Chris turns around to find a place to sit, his close proximity to the long dining table allows him to survey his seating options.

Eager to take advantage of his favorable location, Chris takes his seat adjacent to the head of the table, where the king eventually sits opposite the queen, and princes seat themselves across from the contenders. At each place setting is a very generous repast of shepherd's pie.

The sovereign clears his throat and then announces, "To my guests, let me reward your quest to become a knight on such an august occasion with merriment. The time for battle is nigh. Relax and enjoy this regale before pressing on with your crusade. But I think it's best that you hold off on the libations until dusk!" which is greeted by laughter.

The monarch looks at his nearest guest and says, "It's good to see that you are still here," and then takes a sip from his goblet. "What say you?"

"Thank you for those encouraging words, Your Majesty," Chris says. "Do you think I was crafty enough to find a seat right next to you?"

"As I expected," the king says, "your accent is as foreign as the clothes that you were wearing earlier this morning. Oh, how you flatten the language!" he adds, cringing. As the sovereign drinks from his goblet, his eyes are keenly set upon Chris. Lines of contempt crease the monarch's face. "Crafty?" he asks. "That's a weak comparison to the machinations of my mother and her paramour, Roger Mortimer, who conspired against me. When I was fourteen, he dethroned my father and then became the de facto ruler of England. But almost four years later I seized my rightful place as the Crown of England by leading a coup against Mortimer and later had him executed!" He pounds the table with his fist, rattling everyone's dinnerware.

The conversation around the table stops abruptly. Everyone looks at the king as the queen shoots him a look of disgust.

"Don't mind me," the sovereign says, visibly chastened while he glances at the queen. "My temper got the better of me. Go on," he says to his guests, motioning with his hand, "enjoy your meal."

Slowly everyone resumes eating their lunch.

"Now where was I?" the monarch asks. He returns his goblet to the table and then rubs his eyes with both hands.

Hesitant to answer, Chris bites his tongue.

"Oh yes," the crown says. "What counts today is how well you do in the tournament. By the way, how is your resolution to become mightier and stronger in your quest to attain knighthood?"

"I understand why you see the odds are stacked against me—my slim build and all, Your Majesty," Chris says. "But I seek your help to improve my chances of winning."

"Really? What of your training, if any?"

"That's the subject I would like to discuss with you. There is only one day to prepare for the tournament. If I only had some extra time."

"We all must resolve to be as effective as we can be each day," the sovereign says. "If you're a monarch, then you have to be more productive than commoners."

"Why is that so, Your Majesty?"

"Kings are like stars—they rise and set, they have the worship of the world, but no repose."[51]

Skeptical, Chris asks, "How are you more productive?"

"Through delegation," the crown says and then takes another sip from his goblet. "My father said it best. In fact, it is written on his tombstone." Gesturing to an imaginary gravestone, the sovereign adds, "Here lies a man who knew how to enlist in his service better men than himself."[52]

"All right," Chris says, stroking his chin in curiosity. "Under what circumstances do you delegate?"

"Your time is more valuable than you think," the monarch says. "You need to think like royalty. For example, I have other people clean my room, wash my clothes, cook my meals, and maintain the castle grounds. You can't do it all yourself."

Choosing his words carefully, Chris says, "That can be a challenge for those who don't have access to the same resources as you do."

"You may not delegate as much as I," the king says, apparently not taking offense, "but delegation is still important."

"Then under what circumstances should I delegate?" Chris asks.

"Delegate lesser tasks—those that are beneath you," the crown suggests.

"All right," Chris says.

"In addition to delegating," the sovereign says, "you also have to scrutinize which activities dominate your day. So I prioritize them."

"What are they?" Chris asks.

"Obviously *crises* like wars, treachery, plagues, and pestilence," the monarch says between mouthfuls of food. "I am purely reacting to events as they unfold. The key is to take action now to minimize their occurrence. Accordingly, I spend most of my time planning which alliances to forge, which trading partners to seek, which crops to grow next year, and which bridges to build. And when the harvests are bountiful, England is not at war with France, and the Black Death is in abeyance, I host tournaments and festivals to entertain commoners. Now, if you'll excuse me, I need to talk to the other challengers."

"Absolutely, Your Majesty," Chris says.

Between helpings of food Chris strikes up a conversation with the princes across the table, but it doesn't take long before the meal weighs heavily on his stomach.

The king returns to his seat after he talks to the rest of the competitors individually and enjoys the remainder of his meal. Soon lethargy catches up to the crown as well. With everyone satiated, the sovereign thanks his guests for attending, wishes the contenders good luck during the tournament, and bids them farewell.

* * *

On his way back to rejoin Pierce on the bluff, Chris enters the courtyard. His turbulent day with all the twists and turns makes the pub that he had passed many times earlier seem all the more enticing.

As Chris nears the tavern, the barkeeper calls out in an English tone, "Sir knight, why don't you pull up a chair?"

The apprentice grows silent, mulling it over, and then mutters, "Although I'm not a knight yet, I certainly could use a drink. But I don't know if I have the time."

"Why are you in such a hurry?" the barkeeper inquires.

"Because I haven't finished my training."

"Why do you want to do that? Why not enjoy such a nice day. Take leave of your quest."

"You're right," Chris says. "It seems like I've been practicing for an eternity. I need a break!"

A cold and familiar voice calls out from behind him, "A man is the origin of his action."[53]

Chris turns around and recognizes the sage. "Oh no," the apprentice mumbles.

"It appears as though you've decided to enjoy the rest of this day in repose," the wizard says. "Shirking your training does not reflect well upon your character."

Chris's initial shock gives way to embarrassment. "No, it's not what it seems," he insists. Turning to the barkeeper, Chris says, "Sorry, I need to go. Nice meeting you."

As they leave, the wizard asks, "So, what were the two of you talking about?"

"I was just enjoying a few extra minutes of rest," Chris says with a sigh.

"You are free to do that," the wizard says. "Just remember that for every minute you succumb to a whim or fancy, your training time decreases by that amount." Then he adds, "I have always thought that one man of tolerable abilities may work great changes, and accomplish great affairs among mankind, if he first forms a good plan, and, cutting off all amusements or other employments that would divert his attention, make the execution of that same plan his sole study and business."[54]

"Training is so dull," Chris moans.

"I suppose you had about an hour during lunch to relax from your arduous day," the wizard says. Pointing back to the pub, he adds, "Fate chooses our relatives, we choose our friends."[55]

"What about him?" Chris asks. "He's just tends the bar."

"His profession promotes leisure of the sitting kind," the wizard says. "I would imagine that learning how to wield a long sword and relaxing don't mix." His eyes narrowing, he adds, "Have no friends not equal to yourself."[56]

"Huh?"

"If you want to accomplish great things, consider associating with like-minded people."

"I've heard that before, just phrased differently."

"And here you are consorting with the very kind of people who will delay your preparation for today's tournament," the wizard says.

"Nothing ever becomes real till it is experienced—Even a proverb is no Proverb to you till your Life has illustrated it."[57]

"Well … uh, it seems to be the case that my actions are not following the proverbs," Chris admits. Spotting the proprietor diagonally across the courtyard in the fortune-teller's store, the apprentice exclaims, "Hey! Let's see if my future will change as a result of my progress today. If anyone should know, it would be the fortune-teller. I would like to see him again."

"You know my opinion about their kind," the wizard admonishes. "The last time you saw him, his reaction almost made you believe that you would never win any contest!"

"I just have a feeling that this time will be different," Chris ventures.

The wizard takes a deep breath. Gradually his flinty eyes soften. The sage mutters, "All right," whereupon Chris heads over to the soothsayer's booth.

The apprentice musters some courage and reintroduces himself, saying, "Hi, I am in today's tournament, and I was wondering if I will be the champion."

Looking at Chris suspiciously at first, the fortune-teller waves his right hand across his crystal ball and peers into it. "Funny thing about the future," he says.

"What is that?" Chris asks.

"If I tell you that you are going to win," the fortune-teller explains, "then you will not try as hard, and you might end up losing. Conversely, if I tell you that you are going to lose, then you may not put forth your best effort compared to that if you had not known."

"If you can't tell me about the tournament," Chris says, "can you tell me about my future?"

The fortune-teller gazes into his crystal ball again and says, "All things change, nothing is extinguished … There is nothing

133

in the whole world which is permanent. Everything flows onward; all things are brought into being with a changing nature; the ages themselves glide by in constant movement."[58]

As frustration wells up inside Chris, he says, "But you could have said that to anyone, not just me."

His eyes bearing into Chris, the fortune-teller says, "Yes, that is everyone's future—always in flux—but foreseeing your destiny can alter it because you don't put forth the required effort."

"What kind of fortune-teller are you?" Chris asks. "I could have said that!" Immediately he storms off with the wizard trailing behind.

Once again they amble through the forest, pale against the gloomy sky. The reigning silence provokes Chris's reflection upon the day. *Why was everyone so helpful?* he wonders. *As I discovered firsthand with James, whose agenda am I advancing? Is the king so bored during the apparent peace that he placed a small bet that I would advance through the first round? Perhaps this unknown counterparty includes a member of the royal family—in concert with the jester? Or could it be that this unknown person is one of the jester's friends, as the giant had mentioned earlier?*

With Chris's head spinning from all the possibilities, the two of them return to the bluff where they rejoin Pierce.

As the three meet, Pierce wears an expression of disappointment. "That bloody fool," he grumbles. "The jester told me that you quit after he so easily defeated you."

Chris and the wizard glance at each other.

"Is that true?" Pierce asks.

"Yes, it is," Chris says reluctantly. *Did the jester discern that from afar, or did one of his friends meet Andrew and strike up a conversation with him about my loss?* the apprentice wonders. "But a friend of mine talked me out of it."

The wizard says to Pierce, "Look, I understand that Chris had his misgivings, but I know he is a good person. So please give him another chance."

"All right, but he is running out of opportunities," Pierce cautions. "I do as I please with my time."

"I understand," the wizard says.

Addressing Chris, Pierce asks, "What happened?"

"You could say that the jester was my first opponent in today's tournament," Chris says, "and he defeated me quite easily."

"How did he do that?" Pierce inquires with an upturned palm.

"He used the middle guard while I was using the right-back guard," Chris explains. "Then he charged and tripped me."

"So you didn't use the inside guard to keep him away?"

"No, I didn't. But I was surprised that he charged me."

"Expect to see charging, binding, and tripping during the tournament, among other things," Pierce says, sounding a note of discontent. "Remember the inside guard requires you to hold the hilt at shoulder level with the blade parallel to the ground. That stance allows you to quickly strike your opponent's head, which should make your adversary think twice about moving in and trying to bind you."

"My presence is no longer needed," the wizard interjects and waves good-bye.

Chris does likewise. Thankfully Pierce continues to train the apprentice, who vows that he won't be dissuaded the next time he encounters the jester.

Turning to Pierce, Chris asks, "By the way, how did you and the wizard meet?"

"We met about five years ago," Pierce says. "Apparently something was amiss. He had … lost something."

"You mean a talisman?" Chris asks.

"Oh, so you know?" Pierce says as if a burden had been lifted. "One day I was listening to the town crier, who announced that those people who considered themselves superior in the art of wielding a long sword were requested to assemble in a secluded spot where we were asked to demonstrate our abilities. It was there that I met the wizard. Fortunately he picked me. He told me that I needed to teach a handpicked group of commoners the fundamentals of the craft. The wizard's plan was to establish a fully functional fighting unit—a militia. His instructions were to apprehend the villains behind nearby robberies and lootings and seize the talisman. But he didn't want me to tag along. Just teach."

With a quizzical expression, Chris's mouth starts to gape, and then playing along, he says, "All right." After a few moments of thought, he adds, "I don't understand why the wizard was involved. Why wouldn't the—oh, what's his name?—the *constable* handle such things?"

"I suppose the wizard didn't want the king to worry about some magical item undermining his kingdom. Or perhaps the sage didn't want the charm to fall into the king's hands, and who knows where it would lead from there? Anyway, after the group recovered the talisman, the wizard advised the king to allow me to open up a school to teach commoners the skill of wielding a long sword."

"How does the king feel about this?"

"I'm not sure, but I suppose at least one of my students is a spy to make sure that I'm no threat to the monarchy."

"Oh."

"Anyway, it's time to resume your training," Pierce says. "Let's see how much you remember since you decided to quit."

Chris exchanges his padded long sword for a blunt lying on the table.

Pierce barks, "Left-close guard."

Flummoxed, Chris convulses in fits and starts while he tries to assume the correct stance. Utterly disappointed, he says, "I have been practicing this all day! Why can't I remember it?"

"So you forgot a stance," Pierce says. "Big deal."

"When will I ever learn this?" Chris asks, wondering whether he'll be a colossal failure during the contest.

"Don't forget that you are attempting to learn everything you can about swordsmanship in one day," Pierce says. "That's a lot to ask of yourself."

"I'm so frustrated!" Chris laments. "After thirty years of thinking that I wouldn't amount to anything physically and just recently losing to the jester, how do I get myself motivated and excited to do the things that I haven't done for such a long time?"

"All right," Pierce says. "Certainly one person who overcame disappointment is Michael Jordan."

"Why does everyone always give sports figures as examples?" Chris asks, bridling at the suggestion. "I am forty-one years old with no chance to be in any professional sports league or association, even if I started today. Can I draw inspiration from people who pursued other fields?"

Pierce rubs his temples. Then he adds, "If nonsports examples work for you, I can certainly mention a few. One person who had a challenging life is Bill Porter, who was born with cerebral palsy."

"I've heard of the disease," Chris says, his face grave, "but I am not exactly sure what the symptoms are."

"He had difficulties on his right side of his body, and his speech was slurred. After a four-month job search Porter was told by his employment agency that he would experience greater success collecting welfare than trying to find a job."

"That's terrible advice. I'm sure that he eventually found something."

"Do you think he became a success in life?"

After a long pause Chris says, "I suspect not."

"Each workday," Pierce says, "he took ninety minutes to get dressed in the morning before catching a bus to work, and then he reversed his routine on the way back home. He eventually became a top salesman, and he didn't pretend to be like someone else to disguise his disability."

"I'll take your word for it."

"I have learned that success is to be measured not so much by the position that one has reached in life as by the obstacles which he has overcome while trying to succeed."[59]

"Yes, he's had obstacles in spades. That's a huge personal triumph. Must one have an illness to muster ambition?"

"No, of course not," Pierce says. "That example was meant to illustrate that when fate has dealt *you* a setback, figure out what you can achieve within your limitations and then get on with your life."

"You touched on that subject earlier today when you mentioned that my weapon doesn't care about my past," Chris says.

"You have a good memory," Pierce says, nodding. Abruptly he snaps his head around and stands slightly taller as if his hunting instincts, perhaps long dormant, have come to life. He takes a few steps toward the forest edge, stops, and then shades his eyes briefly with his left hand. He pauses for a few moments and then shakes his head.

"I thought I saw something," Pierce says as he ambles back to Chris, "but I guess my eyes are playing tricks on me."

Chris doesn't know what to make of the situation.

"Anyway," Pierce says, "getting back to your question about inspiration, while being told no to your face by a superior might stop most people, overcoming it and achieving something that had never been done before is truly heartening."

"All right," Chris says, wondering what that could possibly be.

"One such person, rising through the ranks of political office, reached a cabinet-post position as education minister, a level from which an appointed woman could climb no higher. Years passed, and then luck intervened. At the eleventh hour, to her party's surprise, their right-wing candidate bowed out of the election, and she resolved to take his place. When she informed her party chairman of her decision at a later meeting, he told her that she would lose and was summarily dismissed. Perhaps her party chairman's sentiments were anchored in his belief that because no woman had ever been elected to his country's highest office, the status quo would continue. But her eventual victory at the polls proved her critics wrong. Her name was Margaret Thatcher."

"I didn't know about her struggles getting into office," Chris says.

"The secret of success is constancy to purpose,"[60] Pierce says.

"I think that's why they called her the Iron Lady," Chris ventures.

A loud cracking sound rings out from the forest edge. Chris wheels his head around and watches a splintered bough from the middle tier of an aspen tree plummet to the ground, leaving a stranger dangling from two higher branches. Pierce hurries off in that direction. To Chris's surprise, the outsider manages to regain his footing on another lower branch. He hastily descends, shaking a bough with every step. After he drops to the ground, he races into the woods. Pierce pursues the outlier into the forest but returns minutes later.

"Not sure who that was," Pierce says, his face registering vexation. "I couldn't keep up with him because of my armor. Was he a friend of yours?"

"No," Chris says, stifling a laugh. "My friends don't hide in trees. Maybe he was one of the king's spies."

"I doubt that," Pierce says flatly. "The king's agents can keep better tabs on me by attending my classes rather than watching me from afar. Perhaps our spy is one of the other challengers?"

"It wouldn't make sense that another competitor is spying on me because I'm the least of their worries," Chris says. "Maybe the jester?"

"I'm sure you're a better warrior than what you give yourself credit for," Pierce says, patting Chris on his armored shoulder. "Verbal abuse and wielding a long sword are his only strengths. Spying on us doesn't fit into either category."

"All right," Chris says, taking a glimpse of the forest edge. "Then it could be one of the jester's friends as the giant had mentioned."

"That's a possibility," Pierce says, nodding. "Who knows what they're up to? But one thing is for sure. Stay close to me, and you'll have nothing to worry about." Beckoning toward the bluff, he adds, "Why don't we head this way so I won't be tempted to repeatedly glance at the woods to see if our spy has reappeared?"

"All right," Chris says, whereupon the two of them head off toward the palisade.

"Now where was I?"

"Um … something about overcoming setbacks."

"Right," Pierce says. Raising his forefinger resolutely, his hand still sheathed in his gauntlet, he adds, "Another person who overcame huge obstacles pursued a different field of achievement and blazed her own trail, though hers was arguably steeper. To say that she was a disadvantaged youth would be an understatement. She was born to a single mother who was mired in poverty and raised by her grandmother on a Mississippi farm."

An expression of disbelief stretches across Chris's face.

"Her interest in books was encouraged and eventually blossomed. When she was three, she impressed her fellow church members by reading the Bible out loud. Later she was reunited with her mother in

Wisconsin when she was six years old and then lived with her father in Nashville two years afterwards. In the seventh grade, while she was reading a book during lunch, she was spotted by a teacher who helped her secure a scholarship to a better school where her prior experience speaking in front of groups gave her the confidence to enter beauty contests and answer questions with aplomb."

"It sounds like she caught a break," Chris ventures, drawing his gauntlet to his chin, "although I'm not sure whether she escaped poverty."

"We'll see," Pierce says and gives Chris a knowing look. "By the time she reached the age of seventeen, her poise, beauty, and skill led her to be crowned Miss Fire Prevention in Nashville. One of her duties brought her to a local TV station where she was asked to read a news transcript. Impressed with her performance, the station's management hired her! As an undergraduate, her interest in television continued. Surmounting historical trends, she persevered to become the first female and African American anchor at Tennessee State University during her sophomore year."

"That's quite a climb considering that attending college was probably unthinkable when she was growing up," Chris says, wondering whether he could muster the same perseverance if he were in her shoes.

"I agree," Pierce says, nodding. "Although she sought and eventually accepted the same position after graduation, this time in Baltimore, her calling was give-and-take. When a similar opportunity presented itself across the country, she pursued it, hosting *AM Chicago*, which was later renamed *The Oprah Winfrey Show*."

"I had no idea," Chris says softly.

"Certainly she transcended obstacles that would have stopped others—poverty, a fractured home, and a history without representation by women and African Americans in television at her university. And yet she went on to become the most successful talk-show host ever and a philanthropist, among other accolades."

"No doubt her story is inspiring to everyone," Chris says.

"And I hope that includes *you*," Pierce says as they draw up to the precipice that's bordered by hedges. Gesturing to the lake, he adds, "I find the great thing in this world is not so much where we stand, as in what direction we are moving: To reach the port of heaven, we must sail sometimes with the wind and sometimes against it—but we must sail, and not drift, nor lie at anchor."[61]

"I don't face a fraction of the obstacles that she had to overcome," Chris says. He looks at the yawning blue expanse with newfound energy. He turns to Pierce and adds, "I've clung to my childhood issue for too long."

Extending an open hand toward the apprentice, Pierce asks, "So, do you see your future improving?"

"Yes!" Chris says emphatically. "In fact, I told the wizard that I'm interested in mastering the martial arts. After all, that form of combat and wielding a long sword are related."

"There is a certain appeal to inflicting bodily harm on others," Pierce says with a wry smile.

"Or defending yourself," Chris says.

"How many years will it take you to accomplish that?" Pierce asks.

"Quite a few."

"I suppose you'll need to keep your current job until then."

"Yes, but since the two disciplines are so similar, succeeding in the tournament would give me a confidence boost I need to pursue the martial arts."

"I wouldn't stake my entire future on winning the tournament, although it certainly would help."

CHAPTER 10

REFLECTIONS IN THE LOOKING GLASS

"It's time to continue honing your skills," Pierce suggests, "now that you're finally motivated to overcome your childhood setbacks."

"All right," Chris says, looking forward to the remainder of his training.

For an hour under Pierce's tutelage, Chris continues his instruction and then takes a break. He sits on a nearby bench and then closes his eyes to rest his weary soul. But after a few minutes the bench becomes hard and unforgiving much like the day. His unyielding armor doesn't help matters much either. To enjoy his peaceful interlude, Chris listens to the wind streaming through the leaves. Unexpectedly a familiar and disturbing voice right above him says, "I've found the apprentice again. You are daft to leave yourself defenseless yet a second time!"

Instantly Chris jolts his eyes open and sees a looming figure above him. Bolting to the table, Chris retrieves his blunt and brandishes it, ready to strike.

"Save your strength for the tournament," the giant says, taking a few steps backward.

Gazing up at the titan, Pierce says to Chris, "Don't worry about him. He's been very helpful today storing equipment. It's not every day that you have a giant at your disposal. In any event, we need to head back to the courtyard. There's a storm brewing, and there is no shelter here. Make sure you don't forget to grab your other sword!"

"Okay, but I still don't trust him," Chris says with reservation. He lowers his blunt and gazes at the gathering darkness in the western horizon.

* * *

The three enter the courtyard and approach the closer structure on their left, where many amusement games reside. A cacophonous din—raucous carnival barkers, chattering and cheering patrons, and chiming bells—competes for Chris's attention until the giant asks him, "What do you hope to accomplish today?"

"Obviously to win the tournament," Chris says, not giving it much thought.

"Yes, we would all like to finish first in the competition," the giant says, "but adding up the sheer number of competitors, that can't possibly happen to all of them."

"Yes," Chris says, acknowledging reality.

"You should think about success in the following way," Pierce says, addressing Chris. "Don't worry much about trying to be better than someone else.... Always try to be the very best that you can be. Learn from others, yes. But don't just try to be better than they are. You have no control over that. Instead try, and try very hard, to be the best that you can be. That you have control over. Maybe you'll be better than someone else and maybe you won't. That part of it will take care of itself."[62]

"I wasn't taught that at all when I was growing up," Chris says, shaking his head slowly. "It will take me some time to warm up to that idea."

"That's why you need to keep practicing the fundamentals, because you have control over that," Pierce says. Pointing to the device, he adds, "First, we'll gauge your might on the test-of-strength machine."

Chris looks at a vertical scale that has five levels—legend, warrior, laborer, bully, and weakling.

"What level do you think you'll reach?" Pierce asks.

"Bully," Chris says swiftly with a brave face.

"Well, have a go at it," Pierce exhorts.

Chris lays his blunt and helmet on the ground. He adjusts his padded long sword secured to his belt's ring for a few moments and then walks over and picks up the mallet. With a groan, he swings as hard as he can despite his armor, striking the target. With a clang, the weight barely ascends to the upper limits of weakling level and then plummets back to earth. Muttering to himself and disheartened, Chris tramps over to Pierce. The giant in turn strolls over to the machine, grabs the mallet, and swings it with one hand, walloping the target with a tremendous thud. The weight flies up the scale and breaks the bell at the top.

Pointing to the giant, Chris informs Pierce, "I plan to be twice as strong by next week and eventually equal the giant's strength in a year or two. I heard that if someone else can accomplish a feat, then so can I."

"I am also interested in improving your strength," Pierce says, "just not at the accelerated schedule that you just predicted. Were you aware that I have never seen anyone stronger than the giant?"

"I suppose that could be true," Chris muses grudgingly.

"Be content with your lot; one cannot be first in everything,"[63] Pierce says.

"I may never be as strong as the giant," Chris says, "but I won't concede anything else."

"Can you sing?" Pierce asks.

"You got me there," Chris admits.

Nodding, Pierce says, "We'd all like to be stronger, smarter, etc. Most people draw up their plans to do just that in their version of Shangri-la in which resistance doesn't exist."

Chris laughs.

"What?" Pierce asks.

"Of course you brought that up because I was in just in space."

"I'm sure your list of feats was quite impressive."

"Yes," Chris says with pride, yearning to soar again. "I was Superman, but so was everyone else."

"Indeed, it is in that environment in which most people generate a wild number that they think they could accomplish and then find out that they can't do it on Earth … or more appropriately, in real life."

"That's right," Chris says, puffing out his chest. "I could do all the somersaults I wanted to do. I could soar indefinitely. The only thing that stopped me was the confines of the station."

"Are you ready for a different approach then?"

"Absolutely. What is it?"

"I prefer not to dwell in the theoretical. Rather, I think another practical lesson will have a more powerful impact. In fact, the giant has something in store for you right now."

Addressing Chris, pointing between the pub and the small theater, the giant says, "We've tested your strength. Now let's test your stamina. Let's go over to the Human Chess Arena to do that."

"I remember Pierce saying earlier that it involves swinging away at your opponent for minutes on end," Chris says as he gathers his equipment, whereupon the three of them head that way.

Addressing Chris, the giant asks, "How long do you think you'll last?"

"About twenty minutes," Chris ventures.

"How did you come up with that number?" the giant asks, his head cocked to the right.

"I'll need to keep up the pace for twenty minutes overall," Chris explains. "Each round lasts for ten minutes."

"When was the last time you did any vigorous physical activity for twenty minutes?" the giant asks.

"I did something close to that about six months ago," Chris says. "I had to spend at least fifteen minutes on a treadmill without a break to be cleared as a payload specialist."

"What are a treadmill and a payload—" the giant asks.

Addressing Chris, Pierce interjects, "Haven't you learned anything from this morning? I'm not goading you this time!"

"To win the tournament," Chris says, "I'll need to hold up for that long. Besides, I've heard that the first step toward achievement is to aim for a set level of effort."

The giant says to Chris in a disbelieving tone, "I hope you are right. Let's see how long you'll last before you tire out. You'll need your blunt. You will spar with Pierce, only this time it will not be simulated attacks. Rather, it will be full contact!"

Looking at Pierce, Chris voices with concern, "I thought you said there wasn't going to be any full contact using a blunt."

"Yes, I did," Pierce says, "but I'll be limited to defensive moves, and I'm good enough to parry all your strikes."

"I'll take your word for it," Chris says. As he arrives at the alternating colored squares of the Human Chess Arena, he notices a fleet of menacing clouds, portents of a gathering tempest in the western sky growing darker by the minute. He deposits his helmet and padded long sword on the ground between Pierce and the wizard's den—the most likely place for shelter—replaces his sneakers with armored shoes, and readies his blunt.

The giant informs Pierce, "I'll keep track of Chris's time."

Addressing Chris, Pierce says, "I hope we'll be able to finish this. Let's see how long you will last." As he dons his helmet, he adds, "Try every offensive combination you can think of and just keep going. Begin!"

The giant counts off the seconds out loud as Chris swings away at his instructor, who easily blocks all his apprentice's attacks. But what had started out as a vigorous pace soon ebbs until Chris can fight no longer. Doubled over and winded, he whimpers, "That's enough!"

"That was about two minutes," the giant says.

"Hold on!" Chris snarls, gasping for air.

"What you just accomplished was an improvement over the last six months of inactivity," the giant says.

"That appears to be the case," Chris says, his chest heaving.

With a chaotic sky roiling above them, a flash of lightning precedes a rumble of thunder, which echoes off the mountains with chilling effect. A fist of wind lashes their bodies. Pierce tosses his blunt to the ground and exclaims, "Drop your weapon and let's get out of here before we get electrocuted!"

While hastily doing so and then pointing toward shelter, Chris shouts, "Follow me!" Out of the corner of his eye, he sees the giant racing toward the juggler's shop adjacent to the courtyard entrance. Chris initially sprints toward the wizard's door and then rapidly picks up his helmet, which contains his wallet, cell phone, and sneakers. An instant later another bolt of lightning sears the sky, followed by concomitant volleys of deafening thunder. Chris resumes his mad dash and reaches the door first just as rain starts pelting his body. With a quick flick of his left hand, he opens the portal and stumbles inside followed by Pierce.

To the apprentice's astonishment, the wizard is gone, but warmth and shelter are present. Against the far wall the fireplace crackles and hisses, and firelight dances about the room.

Catching his breath, Chris raises his voice above the din of pouring rain pelting the roof and says, "I wonder where the wizard is. He was here earlier today."

"I'm sure he can take care of himself," Pierce says in a calm voice, his breathing barely accelerated from the short sprint, presumably a result of years instructing students. He removes his helmet and places it on the floor and adds, "Maybe he got bored and went someplace else."

"I guess you're right," Chris says as he warily inspects the floor for any sign of snakes. Like Pierce, Chris lays his helmet on the floor as well.

"Sorry your training is interrupted," Pierce says, "but so is everyone else's. At least we have a fire to warm us up."

"Good idea," Chris says. "I could use a break right now."

As the two advance toward the dying fire—a mound of glowing coals—Pierce admonishes, "But it may not be the break you had in mind."

"Oh?" Chris says, caught off guard.

"Let me ask you a few questions about the start of your day."

"All right."

"Tell me about your trip here."

"I flew over in a small plane with an acquaintance," Chris says as the two of them stop abreast of the lectern that's a few feet from the fireplace. "Then we took a cab from the airport here."

"So it sounds like as long as you have a machine to transport you," Pierce says, "your arrival at a selected destination at the appointed hour is virtually assured."

"Yes, but I think I know where you're going with this," Chris says reluctantly.

"Of course you do," Pierce says. "With the help of a machine, you simply guide it in the proper direction or enter your destination in its navigational computer. Without one, your plan becomes dodgy."

"I just come up with a number that I need to attain and then hope my body can achieve it," Chris says.

"Hope is a good breakfast, but it is a bad supper,"[64] Pierce says. "If you can't do it, then what? You hoped to spar for twenty minutes but fell far short. You entered twenty minutes into a machine that bears an uncanny resemblance to your human form, which lacks its own computer to attain the desired results. As you just demonstrated, the best your body could achieve was two minutes. What is plan B?"

"An alternative to my approach is to divide my goal into intermediate or reachable objectives," Chris says, "with the hope of eventually accomplishing it."

"Yes, that approach has a following," Pierce says. "Have you considered others?"

"That's the only one I know," Chris says, shrugging his shoulders.

"The human body can accommodate new demands placed on it over time," Pierce says. "It's the 'over time' part that gives people the most trouble. When you look in the mirror, don't expect to see a machine—one that is able to achieve the desired results immediately or by an appointed date ... or one that improves at the same rate over time until it reaches its design limit. Rather, think of your reflection as an organic structure that has the *potential* to improve, one that is capable of what your muscles can bear, mind can tolerate, and heart can endure."

"Okay," Chris says, not yet convinced.

"What are your thoughts on the following scenario? Rather than hoping that your body can adjust to X level of effort in an arbitrary time period—usually relating to the calendar for some upcoming event—see what results you can achieve on a consistent basis and then seek to improve your efforts from there. The former is time-based. The latter is action-based."

"Since I just failed miserably, I'll try the second approach for now."

"Good," Pierce says. "So from now on we'll focus on action, not time."

"All right," Chris says.

As swiftly as the storm engulfed them, the rain moderates into a soothing pitter-patter above them.

Glancing at the ceiling, Pierce says, "In action-based change, it doesn't matter whether it's improving your might, such as the test-of-strength machine you just tried, or improving your stamina, such as swinging away at your opponent for minutes on end. It's all the same. So the first challenge is to discover what that organic structure of yours can bear right now—what your muscles can handle without shredding them, how far you can run or swing away at your opponent until your body fatigues, etc. All your efforts to improve your strength and stamina will help you—not so much for today's tournament but for future trials and contests. If you become a knight, then developing those two capabilities will help you to fight another day."

Chris rolls his eyes, and in doing so, he spots the wizard's tome on the lectern.

"To determine whether your effort is sustainable, see if you can match your earlier results. If so, you've established a minimum level of effort that you can endure more than once. Otherwise you've overreached and should scale back your efforts by achieving a more modest level of success, one that you'll need to duplicate again."

"That's depressing," Chris says and walks up to the lectern. "If I repeat my two-minute performance, then everyone will know that I'm a beginner. I don't want to be known as the two-minute man."

"Even my best students who eventually became experts started out as novices," Pierce says in a reassuring voice. "They lived to train another day because they didn't become discouraged! They didn't mistake their bodies for machines and believed that they could accomplish a higher number—one that neatly fits into a formula for a day, week, fortnight, or tournament; one that they thought would impress their friends or instructors; or one that matches the giant's capabilities—than what their bodies could handle."

His back to the fire, Chris says, "I see," and gazes down at the wizard's book. Unfortunately the dim firelight, his own shadow, and the tome's old age and worn cover prevent him from discerning the volume's title. No doubt if he held the tome upright against the glow of the fire, he would have all the light he'd need.

"So those two challenges—finding out what you can accomplish and whether you can do so again—shouldn't take you longer than a few days to complete. The reason why you won't do that next is that I need to preserve your energy for today's tournament, considering that you were exhausted running around the grounds this morning and battling me this afternoon. In any event, once you've completed the first two challenges, you are ready to transition from determining what you can do to *improving* upon it."

"Thanks for looking out for me," Chris says. He removes both gauntlets and tosses them to the floor as he prepares to skim through the pages with some dexterity.

"Of course, my intent for you does *not* include learning magic!" Pierce cautions. "Otherwise, why spend all your time preparing for the tournament?"

"Learning magic," Chris scoffs. He traces the edges of the wizard's book cover with his right index finger. *Is this a test to see if I would open it?* he wonders. *Did the old man leave this behind to pique my interest? Maybe the sage had simply forgotten his prop? Assuming that it is a prop, what could possibly be inside that could hold his attention for so long? Perhaps he had inserted between or pasted in pages of personal histories of long deceased relatives, instructions on a new hobby, pictures of lost loves, or long-forgotten journal entries of his youth.* Chris looks at Pierce intently and then ventures, "Oh, I'll bet the book's contents are just a few reflections of a sentimental old man—one especially prone to exaggeration."

"We all have our faults," Pierce says. "Regardless, I'm sure he would like to keep his journal private. I'll bet that even you would like to record your thoughts about your adventure in space. Would you like to have total strangers leafing through your journal?"

"Of course not," Chris says as he rejoins his instructor, facing the fireplace again.

"Good," Pierce says. "Now where was I? Oh, yes, that brings us to the next step, which is to celebrate your success for matching your earlier effort. If it takes you six months to a year to reach your *ultimate* target of twenty minutes of continuous fighting without some kind of payoff, you would never do it."

"Right," Chris says, yawning. The dim light combined with radiant heat and an unbelievably long day makes him sleepy.

"The next challenge is to increase your previous results by a small proportion," Pierce says.

Chris grows silent in contemplation. He extends his hands toward the fire and says, "So once I've sparred for another two minutes without a break, I can look forward to doing so again for three minutes on the next occasion."

Pierce sighs, and his face tightens. Then he says, "That's not what I'd call a small proportion. That would be a 50 percent improvement over your previous effort, which is huge."

"It's just an extra minute," Chris grumbles, lowering his arms to his side.

"Don't treat your body to such abuse by attempting a wild increase over the last effort," Pierce cautions. "Slow and steady wins the race."[65]

"Huh?"

"That's why you should aim for a 5 to 10 percent improvement so that you can find your stride, so to speak."

"Oh, I get it," Chris says. "I'll look for smaller gains then."

"By following these steps," Pierce says, folding his arms, "you can improve your strength and stamina."

"I see," Chris says. "It sounds simple enough." As wrinkles well up in his forehead, he adds, "But how soon can I expect my body to reach the next or even successive levels of achievement? You see, I'm trying to make up for lost time. Will that be a matter of days or weeks?"

"Doesn't that sound like the software code of a *machine*?" Pierce asks, glowering at his apprentice. "Instead your body will adapt to your new endeavor on its *own* schedule."

"Okay," Chris says, nodding slightly.

The sound of the rain finally subsides.

"I think the storm has passed," Pierce says, gesturing toward the door. "It's time to resume your training."

* * *

As the two head outside, Chris beholds towering citadels of condensation borne by summer breezes, floating silently across the sky.

The two gaze at the spectacle for a few moments, and then Pierce leads the way back to the soggy Human Chess Arena. Upon their arrival, the two face each other. Pierce says, "Why don't you continue practicing your stances."

"Sure," Chris says. He points across the courtyard and adds, "Hey, there's the giant."

"Looks like he's okay," Pierce says.

Approaching Pierce, the giant asks, "Is there anything else you need help with today?"

"No," Pierce says. "You are free to go unless you would like to accompany us to see Chris in today's tournament?"

A look of apprehension spreads across the giant's face. "Sorry, I can't. Since the king will be there, so will his guards. They still might want to apprehend me for my crimes committed earlier in life as a brigand. Besides, the wizard isn't around to help me get out of trouble." Addressing Chris, the giant says, "Good luck in today's tournament."

"Thank you," Chris says and firmly shakes the giant's hand. "And good luck with your future endeavors."

"Thanks," the giant says with a pleasant grin.

"Many thanks for all your help today," Pierce says and shakes the giant's hand.

"You are welcome," the giant says before he turns around and heads toward the courtyard gate.

"He's the wizard's problem now," Pierce says softly. "I was only responsible for him until today's contest."

"Whatever," Chris says, glad to get rid of the leviathan.

"Anyway, let's get on with your training," Pierce says.

The two walk over and pick up their wet blunts. To Chris's amazement, the vanguard of visitors filters back into the courtyard.

"Now let's see if you remember the left-side guard," Pierce says.

As if overcome by convulsions, Chris eventually adopts the position several seconds later and then shakes his head slowly. "There is so much to remember," he laments.

"You thought this was going to be easy?" Pierce asks.

Biting his lip at first, Chris says, "No, I just didn't think it was going to be this hard."

"Think of your accomplishments," Pierce suggests. "You are probably the only person at your company who ventured into space. Was that hard?"

"This isn't about going into space," Chris says. "It's about learning swordsmanship. How hard can that be?"

"You're just starting," Pierce says. "It's going to take time to remember the stances."

"But I feel that I should have been ready by now."

"Do you think the other contenders practice a few hours and deem themselves experienced?"

Chris sighs as a gust of wind catches his hair, raking it skyward.

"It's going to take time to become skilled at this craft—longer than one day," Pierce says. "With time, you'll achieve the level of mastery you seek. But some people, especially when given a short time frame, think that they will triumph if they rely on one or two ingredients when the recipe for success calls for many. Make sure you don't make the same mistake as you prepare for the tournament. Don't depend solely on your strength, stamina, quickness, or agility. Don't rely solely on footwork, parries, stances, offensive strikes, or feints. Prevailing calls for all of them."

"I must admit the thought has some appeal," Chris says.

"Toil is the law of life and its best fruit,"[66] Pierce says. "You cannot evade hard work."

"It seems as if I've toiled all day."

"Not only must you work hard today but also in the foreseeable future."

Resigned to the idea, Chris says, "Okay."

"Good," Pierce says as he glances at the visitors walking by. "That's what I wanted to hear. By the way, I think you should check what time it is. You don't want to miss the tournament. What's the time on your mobile?"

Chris walks over and plucks his cell phone from his helmet. "It's 3:32," he says.

"Congratulations," Pierce says, "your training is over. Gather your equipment and follow me. We're headed to the Combat Arena."

After doing so, Chris catches up to Pierce, and the two of them walk over a small bridge spanning a swollen creek. Chris watches a few children tearing up tall grass along the banks, knotting their own grassy boats, and placing them in the deluge one by one, much to their amusement. Chris pauses to watch one such vessel hurtling downstream, which narrowly misses some large rocks until it rounds a bend and disappears from view.

"We must press on!" Pierce exclaims.

Startled, Chris says, "Sorry," and the two of them continue eastward along the path to the tournament.

CHAPTER 11

THE QUEST FOR VALHALLA

As the two approach the Combat Arena on their left, Pierce says, "Good luck!" and climbs into the stands. Chris joins the rest of the challengers, who are all wearing armor, save for their heads, amid the din of the clamoring crowd. Meanwhile, freshening breezes slowly dry the field and animate the flags around the perimeter of a modest stadium during intermittent and strengthening sunshine.

On the far side of the Combat Arena, the royal family and their retinue, flanked by sets of musicians, sit in the royal box on a shaded platform that overlooks the afternoon's festivities.

The blare of the king's trumpets silences the multitude. Ushering Chris and a competitor to the center of the arena, the referee announces, "Good lords and ladies, there will be two first-round matches in today's tournament. In the first contest we have Chris Cole and his opponent, Mark Bambrick. Please welcome them." The audience applauds as the two contenders bow before the king, shake hands, and prepare for battle.

The specter of defeat crawls into Chris's mind because he did lose to the jester after all, but that seems like ages ago. Besides, the crowd's energy lifts the apprentice's spirits.

The referee shouts, "Begin!" and the two challengers edge closer to one another. Out of the corner of his eye, Chris sees the jester, all clad in armor except for his head, facing the audience at the bottom of the stands and brandishing his long sword.

"If there ever was a person so undeserving of being a knight," the fool bellows, "his name is Chris Cole. I challenged him to a fight, and I beat him in less than one minute!" The audience erupts in laughter. "He dwells in a castle in the sky, yet he wants to be a knight. And when I was done with him, he was lying on the ground, staring at the stars!" The crowd roars again. Stretching out his frame on the landing, the jester imitates Chris sprawled on his back. The fool asks, "He doesn't look like a god, does he?" Rolling laughter spills from the stands.

Reacting to the jester's verbal blows, Chris feels stung and lets his guard down for a moment. But when he sees his rival drawing closer, Chris raises his weapon and decides to let it slice through the mountain of criticism, contempt, and scorn heaped upon him. If he defeats his opponent, Chris would inflict more pain upon the jester's soul than he could using his own weapon—or he would at least keep the fool quiet until the next round.

With a grunt, Mark swings first—a downward arc at Chris's left shoulder. But the apprentice readily parries the strike and then ripostes with a slash at Mark's right flank but to no avail, as the stroke is thwarted by a counterparry.

As the two retreat from each other, the jester says, "Striking a pose will not make you victorious," which elicits a few more laughs.

Mark and Chris reengage, and the sound of foam weapons thudding against each other resounds. Through a series of swings and a multitude of feints and counterparries, Mark finally lands the first blow. He strikes Chris on his left flank, which transmits the stinging impact through his armor up his body.

Lowering his weapon diagonally behind him, Mark feigns a vertical strike over his head. An instant later he redirects his padded long sword counterclockwise around his torso at Chris's waist. But with such a sluggish stroke from his rival, Chris has plenty of time to block it. When Mark raises his blade above his head, Chris adopts a countering position, extending his weapon at a forty-five-degree angle behind him toward the ground, his hands a few inches away from his right hip. He readies his padded long sword for a powerful strike or parry if necessary.

After Mark feigns another blow, Chris takes advantage of his opponent's recovery and swings first, wheeling his blade around his right thigh to meet his opponent's late downward arc, which knocks Mark's weapon out of his hands. Stunned, Chris wins!

The apprentice immediately doffs his helmet and shakes Mark's hand.

"What luck you have!" a voice calls out. Turning toward his nemesis, Chris sees the jester's face dissolve into anger. "You won't be so fortunate the next time," the fool admonishes. "Just wait until the next round!" As the crowd politely applauds Chris's first-round victory, the jester spits at the apprentice, but his attempt lands well short of its target. The fool wanders away.

Spotting Pierce at the periphery of the arena, Chris goes to meet him and exclaims, "I can't believe it. I won!"

"You were fortunate," Pierce says, dampening Chris's spirits. "Contests in which a competitor drops his weapon from sword-to-sword contact tend to happen to novices. Just remember that luck is the exception, not the rule."

"I'll take it," Chris says, glad to have any positive outcome.

"Do you prefer to watch the next match?" Pierce asks.

"No," Chris says, trying to conserve his mental energy, "I would just find something else to worry about."

"That's your loss," Pierce says. "I'll watch it instead."

"Thanks," Chris says. He nods and then retires to a changing room underneath the stands. After he removes his foot armor at the doorway, he collapses on a nearby bench. He examines his sore feet and notices blisters developing on each heel—probably caused by his unforgiving foot armor. Glad to have some downtime and fatigued from a phenomenally long day, he sinks his head into his gauntlets and listens to the introduction of the next two competitors followed by intermittent cheers and finally the announcement of the winner.

* * *

Pierce rejoins Chris in the changing room and asks, "How are you doing?"

"Just mentally rehearsing the fundamentals," Chris says.

"Glad to hear it," Pierce says. "I just saw the last match, and the winner likes to bind and knock down his opponent."

"Just like the jester."

"Unlike that fool, your opponent is a lot taller and stronger."

"That's just what I need—a taller and stronger jester!"

"At least he won't have an acid-laced tongue," Pierce says.

"That's comforting to know," Chris says, wondering whether he has any chance to defeat his opponent.

"Anyway, when an adversary tries to bind you," Pierce cautions, "don't let him get too close because a binding move favors the stronger competitor."

"I'll fend him off," Chris says.

"Also," Pierce says, "don't allow your opponent to bind your weapon because he will try to slide the middle part of his blade—the stronger part—up to the tip of yours—the weaker part—and he will have an immediate opportunity to strike you in the head with the hilt of his padded long sword."

"Okay," Chris says.

"Also, don't forget that an opponent's attempt to bind you leaves him vulnerable to blows," Pierce says. "So use the inside guard and look for an opportunity to strike."

"I will!" Chris says, vowing not to repeat the same mistake he made earlier with the jester.

"It appears that your foe has only one trick, and if you can defend yourself against that tactic, chances are his other moves won't be as good," Pierce says. "It is tempting, if the only tool you have is a hammer, to treat everything as if it were a nail."[67]

Chris nods.

Retrieving Chris's armored shoes from the doorway, Pierce says, "I think it's time for you to get ready for the final round of the tournament."

"All right," the apprentice says.

Pierce ambles over to Chris and hands him his footgear.

As Chris attempts to don his right armored shoe, pain instantly shoots up his leg. "Something's wrong," he says.

"What is it?" Pierce asks.

"I don't remember my foot armor being so tight," Chris says. "Let me try putting on the other one." After he jams his left foot into the other shoe, Chris winces, adding, "They're both tight! I don't understand. When I arrived here, they didn't feel like they were crushing both feet."

"All right," Pierce says in disbelief. "What happened when I was away?"

"Nothing," Chris says, searching his memory. "I removed my footgear when I entered this room and sat on this bench with my back to the doorway from the intermission to the end of the second match to decompress."

"Not that everyone needs to keep tabs on their foot armor at all times," Pierce says. "Hey, wait a minute!"

"What?"

"I've never seen the jester wear a suit of armor while entertaining an audience before. That's not his style."

"Okay. But what are you driving at?"

"He was wearing his *armored* shoes."

"He switched my foot armor!" Chris exclaims. "Why does he have such small feet?"

"I'm sorry that happened," Pierce says.

"His footgear can barely accommodate my feet that hurt like hell! I don't think I can continue the tournament."

"If you want to forfeit the match—" Pierce says, his manner despondent.

After a long pause Chris says, "No." Shaking his head, his eyes darting around the room, he vows, "I didn't go through all this training just to forfeit the match." Looking at Pierce with steely resolve, Chris adds, "*I'll* have the last laugh, not the jester."

"Good," Pierce says. "It's time to get ready for your next match."

"All right," Chris says, standing up and grimacing. "Let's go."

* * *

Abruptly the brassy notes of trumpets ring out at the Combat Arena, silencing the crowd. The referee guides the competitors to the royal box.

"My two challengers," the king says, standing up, "it pleases me to watch this match in which your destiny hangs in the balance. As

I mentioned this morning, the champion will have a parade in his honor near the end of the day. Good luck to both of you."

The two contenders, showing obeisance, bow before the king and prepare for the closing round. Addressing the audience, the referee declares, "Chris Cole and his opponent, Roger Oxon, are the final competitors in today's tournament."

After a few moments of silence the referee yells, "Begin!"

Pointing his weapon at Chris, Roger says with contempt, "You were lucky to advance to this round. But it shouldn't take long to dispatch you."

Tired of such derisive remarks, Chris says, "Your taunts are second rate compared to the jester's, and he's a lot smarter too."

"But he doesn't have my strength," Roger says, "and obviously neither do you!"

Approaching his adversary, Roger cocks his padded long sword over his head. In response, Chris raises his weapon before the looming figure. After several feints, each of which elicits a different countering position from Chris, Roger laughs disdainfully and says, "It's so easy to manipulate you." Recoiling from pain, Chris takes a step back and groans.

Finally the first strike is delivered. Roger swings his blade vertically, and Chris easily parries.

Realizing that time is not on his side, Chris begins an offensive volley before Roger has a chance to recover. But for every attack there is a parry and riposte, and for every feint a countering position.

The underdog probes Roger's defenses for weaknesses, but none are detected—at least not yet. Reeling from pain, Chris takes a step back and plants his padded long sword on the ground in front of him, leans over it for a short time, and then slowly raises his guard.

"Too tired to fight?" the jester yells.

"Look at you," Roger says. "You don't even have the strength to stand up."

"It's just an act to fool you into doing something that you wouldn't ordinarily do," Chris says, attempting to sow doubt in his adversary's mind.

Again the larger contender primes his weapon for another strike, raising it over his right shoulder. Instead of a two-handed diagonal swing, which Chris anticipates, Roger wheels his blade using one hand that lacks the former's power and accuracy, which Chris readily parries. The two disengage.

During the lull the jester cries, "Chris, do you expect to defeat your opponent by watching him grow old?" which elicits laughter from the stands. "Come on, Roger. Finish him!"

"The end of the match is nigh, and the advantage is mine!" Roger snorts. "I've trifled with you long enough." With great haste, the imposing competitor rushes toward Chris in an apparent attempt to bind the novice's weapon but is thwarted when Chris assumes the inside guard and delivers a quick strike to Roger's helmet.

Shaking off the blow, Roger barks, "Out of deference to the king, I've let this match last this long, but it's time for you to be vanquished!"

"You're just a two-trick pony," Chris says. "Rumor has it that binding and tripping are your only strengths."

"I've toyed with you long enough," Roger growls. "My next strike will be my last, and I'll cut you into two pieces." His padded long sword held high, Roger charges once more, and with an unbridled and ferocious swing, he pivots his blade down at Chris, who easily wards off the blow. With such vast energy imparted in Roger's swing, his weapon continues its downward arc until it slices into the damp ground, leaving his torso undefended.

Seizing his opportunity, Chris delivers a rising cut that knocks Roger's hands away his partially buried blade. To Chris's amazement, he wins the tournament! He raises his arms in exultation, his mouth agape, and his eyes suffused with glee. The audience erupts with exuberant applause.

The jester slams his hat to the ground and lumbers away. Filling the void, James takes his place, laughing and applauding.

The two challengers remove their helmets and shake each other's hand. As the royal trumpeters play again, the monarch walks out to the middle of the arena and shakes Roger's hand first and then Chris's.

Addressing the winner, the king says, "Great match! Well done. As the victor of the tournament, you have proven yourself worthy of attaining knighthood. What say you?"

Chris secures his weapon and then says, "I would not have won without other people helping me. Thanks to my instructor and … uh, well, the other people who helped and gave me encouragement."

"Yes, but certainly *you* had something to do with it," the sovereign says.

"Well … yes," Chris says reluctantly. "I overcame my self-doubts and a history of inactivity. Also, I learned from my mistakes and how to change."

"That is exceptional," the crown says. "Who knew that the common man had the grit, mettle, and valor to attain knighthood?" Then he adds, "Now for the accolade. Please kneel, Chris." The champion complies slowly, trying his best to minimize his discomfort. The monarch removes his long sword from his scabbard and then, tapping Chris with the flat part of the blade on his left and right shoulder, declares, "By the powers vested in me, during the reign of King Edward III, on this fateful day I dub thee Sir Chris Cole." Then he whispers, "Please stand, Sir Chris."

Chris complies.

"Behold my kingdom," King Edward says. "You are charged with expanding England's sovereignty and protecting her from foreign threats." Turning to the audience, he proclaims, "My loyal subjects, please welcome your new knight!"

Chris is greeted by public acclamation.

"To honor of our most recent champion," King Edward continues, "we will have a parade for him in about forty-five minutes at the King's Court. Please join me in celebrating Sir Chris's victory." The clarion call signals the king's departure.

Smiling, Andrew emerges from the crowd, walks over to Chris, and says, "You didn't give up. Congratulations!"

"Thank you," Chris says. "I am just as surprised as you."

"So when do you want to leave?"

"Can you wait until after the parade?"

"Yes, I can do that," Andrew says. "I could use a parade just about now."

"Great!" Chris says. "Look, I've got to go, but I'll meet you where all three paths converge near the King's Court after the parade."

"Okay, I'll meet you there," Andrew says and takes his leave.

"I saw it coming," a voice calls out behind Chris. After he slowly turns around, he recognizes the fortune-teller, who adds, "You made a lot of progress today."

"I'm amazed that I did."

"Indeed, you overcame your doubts and fears and your illusions that despite being average, you wouldn't amount to much physically."

"I had a lot of help."

"And you sought help."

Chris nods. Anxious to know his fate, he asks, "What is my future going to be like now that I've won the tournament?"

"I need to choose my words carefully because I don't want to alter your future," the fortune-teller cautions. "I can tell you what won't happen. You and your sister will never climb the world's tallest mountain."

Stunned, Chris says, "No, I won't. How did you know that?"

"Some people say I am psychic," the fortune-teller says.

"And I doubted you," Chris says. "But I could have told you that wasn't going to happen to the two of us. The climbing season is so short, and it takes a lot of preparation."

"So," the fortune-teller says, "you can't climb the world's tallest mountain anytime you feel like it."

"But I can climb *my* Mount Everest anytime I want," Chris says.

"If that's what you call it now," the fortune-teller says. "Provided that you follow the guidance that you were given today, you will be a changed man. I am glad you figured that out!"

"But you told me what won't happen in my future," Chris says. "Can you tell me what *will* happen?"

The fortune-teller sighs and says, "I'm sorry, Chris. It's the same as before. If I tell you that you'll succeed, then you won't try as hard and will quite possibly fail. On the other hand, if I tell you that you will fail, then you might not do anything to improve your lot in life." Motioning to the eastern horizon, the soothsayer adds, "Cease to ask what the morrow will bring forth, and set down as gain each day that Fortune grants."[68]

"All right," Chris says, figuring out what the fortune-teller meant. "Then I'll have to quit living in an envisioned future and dwell more in the present. But what must I do *today* to bring about a better tomorrow?"

"Just one thing," the fortune-teller suggests. "If one advances confidently in the direction of his dreams, and endeavors to live the life which he has imagined, he will meet with a success unexpected in common hours."[69]

"Then I would imagine that I'll need to apply all the lessons that I learned today to make that happen."

"Absolutely," the fortune-teller says. "Now, concerning the present, you are scheduled to attend a parade in your honor."

"Yes, I am," Chris says. "See you over there!"

With a nod, the fortune-teller leaves.

But where is the wizard? Chris wonders. *There he is!* Waving his staff above the throng is the sage. Eventually the two meet.

"It appears that you can excel physically after all," the wizard says.

"Thank you," Chris says with a winning smile. "I'm happy that you and Pierce put up with me!"

"Glad to be of help," the wizard says. Pointing to a group of flag bearers leaving the Combat Arena, he adds, "It looks like the parade in your honor will be starting soon."

"Yes," Chris says, "I need to get going. Will I see you again?"

"Certainly," the wizard says. "I will meet you at the King's Court after the parade. Enjoy your victory. You have been waiting a long time for this!"

"Yes, I have," Chris says. "Thanks!"

"See you soon," the wizard says and then disappears into the crowd.

"You might need to wear your sneakers again to walk anywhere," a voice calls out behind him.

"How did you know?" Chris asks facetiously, not bothering to turn around.

"If you had to wear those tiny armored shoes for another minute," Pierce says as he circles around and draws up to Chris, "you'd probably have to crawl on your hands and knees to go anywhere."

"You're probably right," Chris says as he adjusts his padded longsword secured to his belt's ring before sitting on the ground. Gingerly he removes his foot armor.

"Good job," Pierce says as he hands the new knight his sneakers.

"Thank you so much for all your patience and instruction!" Chris says as he lays his sneakers on the ground, removes his cell phone and wallet from his comfortable shoes, and inspects his blister-riddled feet.

"No problem," Pierce says. "Glad to see one of my students rise to the occasion."

"I couldn't have done it without you," Chris says as he begins to put on his sneakers.

Nodding, Pierce says, "Thank you. It's time for me to dash off to the King's Court to find a good spot to watch your parade." Extending his hand, he adds, "Cheers … and good luck with your future endeavors."

"Thanks," Chris says and returns to his feet and shakes his instructor's hand.

"See you over there," Pierce says before he heads off in that direction.

* * *

A phalanx of soldiers, musicians, performers, and mounted dignitaries arrive at the King's Court. To Chris's dislike, a barnlike stench becomes more potent as he approaches them. But his fellow knights, who would easily stand out from the gathering ranks, have not arrived yet. *Perhaps I've shown up too early*, he wonders. Slowly making his way to the rear of the assembly, Chris spots an attendant motioning him to his steed.

When the two meet, Chris says apprehensively, "I've never been on a horse before."

"No problem," the attendant says. "I'll help you up and lash your reins to my saddle."

"But first let me put on my armored shoes for the last time," Chris says, racked by pain as he does so.

Shortly afterward Chris gingerly mounts his horse, helped by his attendant, who then lashes the reins of Chris's horse to his own saddle.

Slowly the two depart the Combat Arena.

This is strange, Chris thinks. *Why are the two of us the only ones moving? Shouldn't I be the last one to go, not the first one? And wouldn't I be riding with the other knights?* As they exit the King's Court, Chris snarls, "Hey, you're heading the wrong way!"

The horse in front murmurs. Looking askance, the mounted attendant says, "I know."

But why would he do that? Chris wonders. *Wait! No doubt his nemesis is behind this.* "I'll bet the jester put you up to this."

Briefly turning around in his saddle, the attendant says in deadpan fashion, "You're catching on."

The thought of yelling, "Help! I'm being kidnapped!" feels distasteful since he became a knight and should be able to fend for himself—even when Pierce is no longer by his side. While the formal contest is over, surely the jester is spoiling for another round.

For a short while they head west and traverse a small bridge over a narrow, frothy stream, whereupon they leave the path and head north into the woods until they meet the jester who is encased in armor, save for his head. He stands near the edge of a slope that spills into a nearby brook.

Looking intently at the blade of his weapon, the jester says calmly, "Well, well, well. The pseudo knight whose skills I find wanting."

"I won the tournament fair and square," Chris says. "I'm not sure why you're in armor. I don't have to fight you."

"I can't believe that you somehow managed to stave off defeat during the tournament," the jester says, lowering his weapon and glowering at Chris. "I'm sorry to hear that you don't want to fight me again. Evidently I wasted a great deal of time preparing to battle you a second time."

Chris scoffs.

"Oh, I forgot to mention this," the jester says as he saunters up to Chris on his horse. "If you want to attend your own victory parade, then you'll have to best me. It would be a pity if you couldn't attend. What would King Edward and all the commoners waiting for you at the parade think?"

"What would he think if he learned that you were the cause?" Chris asks, not taking the threat seriously.

"Revenge has its own rewards," the jester says, turning his back to Chris. "My cost will be that I'll have to leave this kingdom before the monarch finds out."

"Sounds like you'll be hiding for a long time," Chris ventures.

"I think not. I've replaced a jester before, and I can easily do so again in another kingdom." Turning around and facing Chris again, the jester hisses, "Too bad your luck is about to run out yet again today."

"You don't have to do this," Chris says. "I'm just a visitor. I'll be leaving after the parade."

"Why should I believe you?" the jester asks. "When you miss your own parade, you'll be an outcast in the shire!"

No doubt attending the procession will be Chris's just reward for all his hard work. Winning the contest and not being able to celebrate it proves too much for him to fathom. Resigned to the idea of fighting again, Chris dismounts his horse and whimpers as each foot touches the ground. Regaining his composure, he asks, "Is that my foot armor you're wearing?"

"Yes, and they are still too big. Are those mine?"

"Yes, I'm still wearing them. Let's trade."

"All right. But it still won't change the outcome."

"Whatever."

Chris removes his cell phone and wallet from his helmet and lays them on the ground. The two adversaries exchange their armored shoes, don their helmets, and prepare for battle. A cool breeze riffles the treetops above them, sending a shower of red and gold leaves fluttering back to the earth.

As the two close in on each other, Chris realizes that his opponent's weapon is different from his own. "Wait!" he admonishes. "Your sword isn't padded, and your weapon has sharp edges and a pointed tip. It's not dull and rounded like a blunt. You have a long sword. You could seriously injure someone with that! It's too dangerous for me to fight."

Shrugging, the jester says, "Now that you've unexpectedly attained knighthood, if you choose not to fight for your own safety, I'm sure everyone at the parade would understand that your absence is a just one."

His mouth agape, Chris utters no words. The thought that he could miss his flight back to the base from his delay at the hands of the jester dawns on the new knight. However, that is not reason enough to justify the risk of significant injury. "I will not fight you," Chris says defiantly.

"You might want to reconsider because I will exact my revenge upon you! Yours will be a lasting defeat, one that will be etched in your mind for the rest of your life!"

Quickly the two engage. The sound of metal partly slicing through duct tape–wrapped foam abounds. But with such an inferior weapon compared to the jester's, Chris is limited to parries. He tries his best to minimize the angle at which he parries the fool's weapon to reduce the damage inflicted on his own. With his blister-riddled feet still causing him agony, Chris tries to keep his footsteps to a minimum.

The jester lowers his guard, apparently inviting an attack. Chris steps back, not sure what to make of it. Hastily he guesses that the jester wants him to make the same mistake Roger made. So Chris maintains his stance and doesn't take the bait.

Again the jester attacks, but with so many cuts on Chris's padded long sword, a chunk of foam falls to the ground, lightening his weapon.

"It seems like my odds are improving," Chris ventures. "I can wield my weapon faster than you can."

"That doesn't matter since your feet are getting worse with every step you take," the jester says. He then charges Chris, possibly in an attempt to bind, trip, or deliver a blow with the handle of his weapon.

Grimacing, Chris fends off the attack. He assumes the inside guard and then delivers a blow to the jester's helmet.

Taking a step back and then shaking his head briefly, the jester snorts, "Unlike Roger, I'm patient enough to let your feeble feet cost you this battle and your parade."

In reality, the jester is right. A war of attrition is a contest that Chris has no hope of winning. But he didn't invest all this time and energy for naught. Somehow, someway, he'd find an answer.

The jester attacks again, possibly trying to take advantage of close quarters and maneuvers Chris against a tree. Sensing the jester's intentions, Chris circles away, and in doing so, he emerges from the forest's edge onto a wet, leafy slope. As he steps backward, his feet slip out from under him, and he tumbles down the grassy slope, stopping just short of the stream.

Pressing his attack, the jester goes after Chris but loses his footing as well and topples down the hillside.

The two swiftly gather their weapons and reengage.

With his heart racing and his forehead beading with a sheen of sweat from exertion, not to mention the lack of ventilation from being encased in a metal skin, Chris hopes to get the better of his adversary by saying, "Thus far, my skills are equal to yours. Your boasts of your talents being superior to mine are mere fantasy."

"Except for one blow," the jester snarls, "those are mighty words for someone who has been limited to parries." He resumes his attack, forcing Chris to retreat into a shallow stream, one that rises to his shins and is no more than fifteen feet wide.

The jester declares ominously, "Say good riddance to your parade," and grunts as he slaps the stream with the flat side of his blade, sending a spray of water through Chris's faceplate and into his eyes.

As Chris stumbles backward, temporarily blinded, some of his foot blisters break and the resultant pain wells up like molten lava, tempered by the cold mountain water. The sound of the jester's feet sloshing toward him compounds his fear. Without alternatives, Chris holds his weapon with all his might, raising his guard before an unseen enemy. He steels himself against long odds until he can regain his vision, hoping for the best. With another groan, the jester knocks Chris's weapon from his hands. Powerless, Chris feels what's most likely the sharp of the jester's long sword pressing upon his breastplate.

"So, how does it feel now that your luck has come to an end?" the jester howls. "You're certainly not a knight, just an apprentice clad in armor!"

How could this be? Chris wonders. *How could it all be for naught?* Opening his visor, still dripping with water, he sees his worst fear realized.

"I don't think King Edward will throw another parade in your honor. In fact, he might just throw you in the dungeon out of sheer embarrassment. I'd hate to be you right now," the jester—now helmetless—says as he pushes Chris back slightly with the tip of his long sword.

Perhaps out of hubris, the jester extends his weapon toward Chris with only one hand. Laughing, the fool says, "The end of your hopes and dreams is nigh. When darkness falls, the parade will be over. What do you have to say for yourself, errand boy?"

Indeed, just as the wizard foretold this morning, today would be a defining point in Chris's life. And one that Chris would not leave unfulfilled. With a surge of adrenaline coursing through his body, Chris swings his right armored forearm against the jester's long sword, forcing it aside momentarily. Chris takes two steps forward as he unleashes a primal yell and tackles the jester, sending the two of them tumbling into the water. His face submerged, the jester desperately wrestles Chris briefly with one hand. But it doesn't take long before the fool releases his weapon. Chris allows his foe another gasp for breath and then submerges the jester's head again for about fifteen seconds for good measure. Finally Chris releases him.

As his nemesis gasps for breath again, Chris gathers the two submerged weapons. In short order, the cadence of horse's feet splashing upon the silt-bottom shoals of the brook draws Chris's attention. Looking upstream, he sees the falconer on horseback headed his way.

The jester's accomplice flees the area on a whinnying horse.

"I could have used your help earlier," Chris says as the falconer draws near. "What took you so long?"

"Sorry," the falconer says, "I was late in joining the assembly for the parade. By the time I found my place, I realized that you were missing from the group. When I saw you were being led out of the King's Court, I threaded my way through the participants again. I tried to follow you as best I could, but I eventually lost sight of you. So I raced on my horse west to Fun, Food & Drink, but I saw no sign of you along the way. When I headed back in the other direction and arrived at a small bridge, I saw the two of you battling in the stream. So here I am. It looks like you have everything in hand."

"Yeah," Chris says, still breathing hard.

"We still have time to join the parade," the falconer says. "Climb aboard." After Chris does so, the falconer extends his left arm toward the forest edge, prompting his raptor to pitch from a nearby tree limb, sweep dangerously close to the stream, and with its wings outstretched and then fluttering, alight on its master's gloved hand.

Taking one last look at his archenemy, who stands despondently in the brook, Chris says, "If I were you, I'd start running right now."

* * *

The waning sun extends the tree shadows, and the day grows colder at the King's Court.

To rousing fanfare, the procession rapidly surges forward. Music fills the air as flag bearers pass by the royal court followed by drummers and then assorted minstrels. For the visually inspired, acrobats and fire-breathers delight the crowd with leaps and tumbles and an occasional fireball cast skyward. Following them are marching troops, some of whom carry crossbows, longbows, and pole arms of every kind.

The falconer on horseback followed by the king's mounted knights pass by the sovereign next. Bringing up the rear is their most recent addition, Chris, whose horse's reins are lashed to the knight's saddle in front of him. Still donned in armor and carrying his helmet with one hand, Chris waves to King Edward with the other and then to the appreciative crowd. At the end of the parade Chris circles back.

With the culmination of the day's events finally over and the noise of the multitude subsiding, Chris remains jubilant, for he had slain his own doubts and fears, and most importantly, he had escaped from a prison of his own making.

* * *

Dipping below the horizon, the crimson sun kindles a deck of lingering clouds in the western sky.

The falconer's horse guides Chris's steed in tandem along the wide field of the King's Court. Soon Chris spots the wizard alongside a stranger.

When Chris approaches within earshot, the sage says, "You can dismount here. My acquaintance can return your horse to the stables."

Quickly the falconer hands the reins of Chris's horse to the acolyte on foot. The new knight gingerly dismounts, his muscles fatigued and his foot armor bloodstained from the day's events.

Murmuring, his mount is led away.

"How is your kingdom faring now?" the wizard inquires.

"It's many times larger than it was this morning," Chris says with contentment. Realizing that the end of his journey is near and that this will probably be the last time he sees the wizard, Chris adds, "But I wish I'd come here years earlier. I could have been that much further along."

"You put too much emphasis on days gone by," the wizard says. Motioning to the eastern horizon, he adds, "The past is but the beginning of a beginning, and all that is and has been is but the twilight of the dawn."[70]

After Chris takes a few moments to digest that thought, he says, "Okay. I can't dwell on what I could have done in the past, based on what you just said, and as the fortune-teller pointed out, I can't count on my tomorrows either. So what I do in the present is crucial."

"I'm glad you are coming up with your own answers now," the wizard says with a broad grin. "I suppose the reason you've made such strides today was that you started out at the foothills and steadily improved your skill set to scale the mountain rather than mimicking an expert who has already reached the summit."

"Exactly," Chris says, nodding. "Hey! How did you know that?"

"Pierce told me," the wizard says.

"Oh," Chris says, caught by surprise. "Well, thank him for me."

"I just wanted to say congratulations before leaving," the falconer interrupts, still on horseback.

"Thank you. But I wouldn't have succeeded without the wizard's and Pierce's help ... and your assistance as well. If you didn't introduce me to the wizard, my victory wouldn't have been possible."

"Thank you," the falconer says. "It's about time for me to retire this bird for the night. Good-bye, Chris!"

"Good-bye," Chris says in kind.

The falconer takes his leave.

Looking to the east, the wizard says, "The day is drawing to a close, and you no longer need my help."

"Thanks so much for your guidance," Chris says, "especially after I quit so many times. So, what do you think my future holds without your assistance?"

"Don't worry," the wizard says. "You'll manage just fine. Although your struggles for the day are over and you have achieved knighthood, the trials of life continue, particularly now that you have chosen a new field of endeavor." With a knowing look, he adds, "The longest journey is the journey inwards of him who has chosen his destiny."[71]

After much thought, Chris nods.

"Night is almost upon us," the wizard says. Motioning to the path, he adds, "It's time for us to head back."

Chris looks over his right shoulder to get a final glimpse of the Combat Arena, where he had triumphed in glory and, according to King Edward, had changed his destiny. As they slowly make their way toward the path that would deliver Chris from this world to the next, he relishes the day's victories. But his painful feet are too much for him to bear. "I need to remove my foot—" he says.

"Dear God," the wizard interjects, his pace slowing. "I will have to cast some magic after all."

"Oh, great," Chris says, halting abruptly and looking woefully at his foot armor. "*Now* you want to cast a spell. What is it?"

"Do not forsake what you have learned today," the wizard says with mounting concern. Sensing his mentor's anxiety, Chris looks at the wizard, whose skyward gaze prompts the new knight to shift his own attention likewise.

To Chris's horror, darting underneath the bloody clouds appears the sage's nemesis—a rakish silhouette of fear as old as time! An immense dragon banks suddenly and then streaks toward them, growing ever larger in the sky.

"Oh my god!" Chris gasps and immediately drops his helmet by his side.

The wizard braces his body and hefts his staff. He conjures, "Let a great shield protect us!"

Quickly the horned and scaled colossus slows its momentum with a few powerful flaps of its wings and spews a jet of fire directly at their exposed position. Chris reflexively covers his face with one hand and his torso with his other. But the flames are redirected by an invisible dome above them!

His eyes squinting from the intense glare and mounting heat, Chris hears the wizard shouting above the hiss of the fire, "Goodbye, Chris!" and then disappears in the brilliance.

Before Chris has a chance to locate the sage, the conflagration around him changes hue to a pink-purple tint and then recedes into the background as the space shuttle's gray cockpit, bristling with instruments, materializes in the foreground.

The fact that Chris is on the orbiter once again is at odds with his recent medieval fair visit. But a raging ache crowns his skull. He instinctively reaches up to gauge his wound. As he runs his fingers through his hair, a look of astonishment fills his features, for he is the only crew member on the flight deck who is not wearing his pumpkin-colored pressure suit, helmet, and gloves yet again! Indeed, his quest to become a knight was a dream, and he pounds his seat in disgust. Not only is Chris angry that all his hard work in his dream was for naught, but he's also dejected that he didn't have a chance to deploy his experiment. Yet, with the wizard's help, escaping certain death from their fiery encounter with the dragon softened the blow. If the sage had battled the dragon before, he certainly must have found a way to defy the demon.

Chris's headache, however, beckons reality. Still suffering from the effects of a concussion, he barely remembers boarding the space station. He takes a few moments to find a wireless headset and then puts it on.

"This is Chris," he says while he is keying his headset. "What happened?"

"Chris, it's great to hear that you've regained consciousness!" Brian says. "You hit your head against a hatch, and the rest of the crew threaded you back to the shuttle. We tried to wake you up but couldn't, and Mission Control told us to bring you home. The space station's two right main solar arrays have been damaged from space debris, but the remaining solar panels are providing sufficient electricity to the ISS. How are you doing?"

"Oh, I whacked my head pretty good," Chris says. "I've got a major-league headache. Don't worry. I'll recover."

Quickly the spacecraft's fiery reentry ends, yielding to the tranquil aura of twilight, which rapidly fades to night, and its attendant astral lights. It had been a long day for Chris. The nocturnal splendor and his concussion-induced grogginess weigh heavily upon his eyes.

Before sleep overtakes him, his disappointment about his failed mission ebbs as he remembers with gratitude those who helped him on his quest to become a knight, and he vows to use their methods from this day forward.

Returning to Earth's embrace, hurtling in a celestial ship across a vast sea toward an unseen continent on the far side of the world, Chris revels in the wondrous starry night before he slowly drifts back to the land of yore, but he awakens suddenly when the spacecraft lands with an emphatic jolt.

And as one journey come to an end, so another adventure begins anew.

Author Note

Here is a special note from the author, who has chronic Lyme disease:

To help us find a cure for chronic Lyme disease, please consider donating to any one of the following institutions by referencing the websites below:

Columbia University Medical Center, Lyme and Tick-Borne Diseases Research Center	http://www.columbia-lyme.org/donate.html
International Lyme and Associated Diseases Society	http://ilads.org/ilads_media/lyme-challenge/
Lyme Disease Association, Inc.	http://www.lymediseaseassociation.org/index.php/donations
LymeDisease.org	https://www.lymedisease.org/get-involved/donate/
Global Lyme Alliance	http://globallymealliance.org

ENDNOTES

1   Seneca, *Thyestes.*
2   William Shakespeare, *Twelfth Night.*
3   Ralph Waldo Emerson, *Society and Solitude.*
4   Confucius, *Analects.*
5   Theodore Roosevelt, *The Strenuous Life.*
6   Leonardo da Vinci, *The Notebooks.*
7   Publilius Syrus, *Maxim.*
8   Herodotus, *Histories.*
9   Horace (Quintus Horatius Flaccus), *Epistles.*
10 Marcus Porcius Cato (Cato the Elder), *From Caius Julius Victor, Ars Rhetorica.*
11 Ralph Waldo Emerson, *The Conduct of Life.*
12 Horace (Quintus Horatius Flaccus), *Epistles.*
13 Eleanor Roosevelt, *This is My Story.*
14 Johann Wolfgang von Goethe, *Faust: The First Part.*
15 Henry David Thoreau, *Walden.*
16 George Herbert, *Jacula Prudentum.*
17 Sallust, *Speech to Caesar on the State.*
18 Aristophanes, *Wasps.*
19 Ralph Waldo Emerson, *The Conduct of Life.*
20 Mencius, *Works.*
21 Aesop, *Fables.*
22 Euripides, *Alexander.*
23 Philip Dormer Stanhope, earl of Chesterfield, letter to his son.
24 Terence (Publius Terentius Afer), *Heauton Timoroumenos.*
25 Jean de La Fontaine, *Fables.*
26 Euripides, *Hippolytus.*

27   Benjamin Franklin, *Poor Richard's Almanac.*

28   Sophocles, *Oedipus Rex.*

29   Ovid (Publius Ovidius Naso), *Metamorphoses.*

30   Mark Twain (Samuel Langhorne Clemens), *Pudd'nhead Wilson.*

31   Confucius, *The Doctrine of the Mean.*

32   Thomas Cole, *Essay on American Scenery.*

33   Thomas Hardy, *The Mayor of Casterbridge.*

34   Titus Maccius Plautus, *Mostellaria.*

35   Reprinted with the permission of the National Geographic Society from the book *Everest: Mountain Without Mercy* by Broughton Coburn. Copyright © 1997 National Geographic.

36   Ibid.

37   Ralph Waldo Emerson, attributed.

38   Titus Maccius Plautus, *Miles Gloriosus.*

39   Henry Wadsworth Longfellow, *Hyperion.*

40   J. Paul Getty, Archival Playboy Magazine material. Copyright © 1961 by Playboy. Used with permission. All rights reserved.

41   William Shakespeare, *Hamlet.*

42   Samuel Smiles, *Self-Help.*

43   Oscar Wilde, *Lady Windermere's Fan.*

44   Thomas Paine, *The American Crisis.*

45   Miguel de Cervantes, *Don Quixote.*

46   Ovid (Publius Ovidius Naso), *Ars Amatoria.*

47   Benjamin Franklin, *Poor Richard's Almanac.*

48   William James, *The Principles of Psychology.*

49   Plato, *Apology.*

50   George Savile, marquess of Halifax, *Political, Moral, and Miscellaneous Reflections.*

51   Percy Bysshe Shelley, *Hellas.*

52   "[Andrew] Carnegie Wrote His Own Epitaph: 'A Man Who Knew How to Enlist in His Service Better Men Than Himself,'" *The New York Times.*

53   Aristotle, *Nicomachean Ethics.*

54   Benjamin Franklin, *Autobiography.*

55   Jacques Delille, *Malheur et Pitié.*

56   Confucius, *Analects.*

57   John Keats, letter to George and Georgianna Keats.

58 Ovid (Publius Ovidius Naso), *Metamorphoses.*

59 Booker T[aliaferro] Washington, *Up from Slavery.*

60 Benjamin Disraeli, earl of Beaconsfield, speech, June 24, 1872.

61 Oliver Wendell Holmes, *The Autocrat of the Breakfast-table.*

62 Coach John Wooden with Steve Jamison, *Wooden: A Lifetime of Observations and Reflections On and Off the Court* (New York: McGraw Hill, 1997), 169. Used by permission of the McGraw-Hill Companies.

63 Aesop, *Fables.*

64 Francis Bacon, *Apothegms.*

65 Aesop, *Fables.*

66 Sir Lewis Morris, *The Ode of Perfect Years.*

67 Abraham Maslow, *The Psychology of Science.* Copyright © 1966 by Abraham H. Maslow. Copyright renewed 1994 by Bertha G. Maslow. Reprinted courtesy of HarperCollins Publishers.

68 Horace (Quintus Horatius Flaccus), *Odes.*

69 Henry David Thoreau, *Walden.*

70 H. G. Wells, *The Discovery of the Future.*

71 Excerpt(s) from MARKINGS by Dag Hammarskjold, translation copyright © 1964, copyright renewed 1992 by Alfred A. Knopf, a division of Random House LLC and Faber & Faber Ltd. Used by permission of Alfred A. Knopf, an imprint of the Knopf Doubleday Publishing Group, a division of Random House LLC. All rights reserved. Any third party use of this material, outside of this publication, is prohibited. Interested parties must apply directly to Random House LLC for permission.

CPSIA information can be obtained
at www.ICGtesting.com
Printed in the USA
FSOW02n1744101115
13201FS